Your Soul to Take

Rise of the Fallen
Book Two

Sean Hayden

∞ Untold Press ∞

YOUR SOUL TO TAKE

First Untold Press Printing July 2014

Published by Untold Press LLC
114 NE Estia Lane
Port St Lucie, FL 34983

www.untoldpress.com

ISBN: 978-0692256084

PRODUCED IN THE UNITED STATES OF AMERICA

10 9 8 7 6 5 4 3 2 1

Dedication

For the stars of this book, Connor and Caelyn. And I'm not talking about the Sullivan siblings. This book is for my own Connor and Caelyn Hayden. They are the true stars. I love you with all my heart.

Acknowledgements

Special thanks to Dayanara Nijhove-Anthonissen for her help with the cover design!

I would also like to thank my awesome proofreaders: Lynn, Dori, Rayna, Liz, and Angela (even though she took forever!)

Prologue

Be careful what you wish for. We've heard it a million times. Hell, I'm only fifteen and I've heard it my whole life. The problem is nobody *sits you down* and tells you why you should be careful. If they had, my life and the lives of those around me might have turned out completely different.

One minute I was doing homework and minding my own business. The next, I'm writing a promise in my own blood to give my soul to whoever grants my fondest wish. I even remember laughing at the stupidity of it…until I lit that promise in the flame of a black candle and demons showed up to take me up on my offer.

Then all hell broke loose.

See what I did there?

There were three million things I should have wished for. I probably should have just let them take my soul right then and there. Not only would I have been better off, but so would everyone else. I should have wished to be rich, lived a long normal life without any financial concerns, and then spent an eternity in hell's mailroom. But *no.* I had to try and be clever and save my soul. In a moment of panic, I wished to be one of the demons.

As it turns out, the demons, or Fallen as they prefer to be called, aren't that bad. In fact, they're the good guys. The angels on the other hand, like to be called the Chosen and are a bunch of self-righteous pricks. Go figure. At least I picked the cool side.

Being a demon wouldn't be half bad either, if I could have been a normal, tempt you into selling your soul, winged and horny type. I couldn't even get that right. They had to accidentally turn me into some sort of super demon who reminds all the other angels and demons of...you guessed it...The Usurper. That's their fancy name for the big bad guy himself, Lucifer. Turns out he wasn't as bad as everyone thinks. He was just fighting for humanity's free will. The angels don't like that. They want earth to be a utopian society under their rule. Told you they were a bunch of pricks.

What about God?

As it turns out, he is very much real, but has taken a "don't interfere" stance. Looking back through history, I don't blame him. Humans can be quite thick-headed and stubborn. Every time he tried to interfere...it didn't end so well. Just ask Noah.

So where does that leave humanity?

In the same place it's been since the Usurper tricked Eve into taking a bite. On their own. On their own to live and learn, love and hate, and make their own triumphs and failures. I think it's kind of like sending your kid to college. They're either going to pass out doing keg-stands, flunk out, or muddle through with a C average and get a mediocre job, or blow their GPA through the roof and run for some sort of office.

I mentioned I was a freak among demons, but I didn't say why. I started out low man on the totem pole. I was what you would call a Seeker. Basically, I find people who were like me, willing to sell their soul for the lure of anything they wanted. I did my job and I did it well. Too well. There was a teenager named Brett who wanted to be a vampire more than anything in the world. I granted his wish. I turned him into a freak, too. He was more powerful than a locomotive and could throw people over tall buildings with a single arm. He was *way* stronger than he should have been. He kicked my ass several times, and was even too powerful for Darius, the leader of the Reapers, to take his soul.

If that weren't enough for a young teenage boy turned demon to deal with, fate decided to throw me a curveball. A five-foot-two-inch curveball with red hair, freckles, and green eyes. My little demon heart didn't stand a chance. I was hooked instantly.

What's the problem?

Know the sworn enemies of us demons? The Chosen I mentioned earlier? As it turned out, her father was one. Too good to be true doesn't begin to cover it.

But wait, there's more. See Jessie quickly took a liking to me, too. It's almost as if we were destined to be together despite the very serious differences in our lineage. But as it turns out, Jessie was only *half* Chosen. Her mother was human. Bad things happen when Fallen and Chosen mate with humans. Very bad things. Their children are doomed to suffer as humans for their very short lives. At the time of their death, they are either strong enough to become fully Chosen, or their souls are banished to the otherworld. That's the mailroom in hell I mentioned earlier. Never been there, but I'm sure it's lovely this time of year.

To top it all off, my girlfriend was kidnapped by the vampire I created, I had to ask her father to help me rescue her (let's just say he wasn't too happy with me), and I had to defeat the vampire all on my own.

I did it, but at a horrible price.

The life of my sister.

Chapter 1

I must have cried myself out. The tears stopped falling and I breathed in through my nose. I stood up and looked down at my baby sister lying there. I kissed my fingertips and touched her forehead.

"Goodbye, brat," I whispered.

"Stop calling me brat."

Caelyn's eyes opened. Her irises were blood red. She gave me an impish smile and bared her fangs.

Little sisters suck.

I should have felt five million things, relief that my sister was still alive, sort of, being the foremost. The only thing I could *really* think about was how to tell my parents. *Um…Mom, Dad, your daughter's a vampire…*Yeah, that probably wouldn't go over too well. As awkward as it was, I reached down and hugged her for all that she was worth.

"Are you insane? Get off me!" She squirmed in my hug and got her hands on my chest. When she tried to gently push me away, she ended up throwing me halfway across the room. I skidded to a stop on the linoleum floor without crashing into anything. Caelyn sat up on the morgue table with a horrified look on her face. "What just happened?"

She looked around and knew. She knew where she was and why she was there. She stared down at her hands. Sure enough, she'd grown talons just like Brett had when he became a vampire. Caelyn knew exactly what she was, but the look she gave me begged for me to tell her something different, that she was wrong.

I couldn't. I gave her a slow nod, confirming her fears and completely destroying the last bit of hope she might have had.

My sister and I hadn't gotten along since she was two. Giving her horrible news had always been one of my favorite recreational sports. *Hey, Cae, Mom found that test you were trying to hide. Hey, Sis, Dad found out you kissed Chuck.* That sort of thing had given me more satisfaction than my PS3 *ever* had. Unexpectedly, that one simple nod, telling my sister her worst fears were true and that she was a vampire, made me feel a little sick to my stomach. "Cae, I…"

Her face crumpled into a mask of anguish. I heard the first tear hit the metal table beneath her before the first sob escaped her lips. I was back across the room before the second one fell. The first hug I had given my sister was awkward. She didn't want me hugging her. This time she collapsed in my arms and accepted it. Maybe even needed it.

"What happened?"

Her question kind of threw me off guard. "We thought you were dead," I said, thinking she meant how she ended up in the morgue.

"I swear, Mom and Dad dropped you when you were a child. I *know* why I'm here. I meant why am I alive? Why do I have talons? Am I a vampire like that asshole who broke into the house? Am I going to stay this way? What am I going to do now? More importantly, what the hell are you? I saw you! You had wings? Connor…"

"Wait! Slow down," I said and pulled away. I leaned against the table and she tightened the sheet around her. "I don't know how you became a vampire. I'll be honest. It's not supposed to happen that way, but I'm glad it did. I'd rather have a fangy sister than no sister." I gave her a little smile and she rolled her eyes. Typical Caelyn.

"What do you mean it's not supposed to happen that way?"

"Vampires. What happened wasn't how it was *supposed* to happen. Somebody can wish to become a vampire, but they can't make anybody else a vampire against their will. It doesn't work like that."

"What doesn't work like that? What the hell are you talking about and more importantly, what the hell did they turn you into?"

Dad's cough from outside the door stopped our conversation.

"Listen, Cae. I promise to tell you *everything* as soon as we get out of here and I figure out what to tell Mom and Dad."

She nodded and wiped the tears rolling down her cheeks with the back of her hand. "Okay."

I needed help. "Stay right here. Play dead," I added with a small, sad smile that actually made her give a short bark of laughter.

"I think I can manage."

I nodded and made my way to the morgue room doors. I glanced through the window and saw Dad standing in the hallway looking like... Well, looking like his daughter had just died. I pushed the door open and he looked up from the floor. "You ready to go, Connor?"

"Dad," I said and looked him right in the eye. "You need to wait here for a moment. Do *not* go into the morgue." I used my power just like Clarisse had taught me to. He would obey. He didn't have a choice. His eyes glazed over and he stared straight ahead.

I ran through the halls of the hospital to the waiting room where I'd left Clarisse and my mom sitting and crying. Clarisse saw me–or felt me–as soon as I entered the room. I gave her a panicked smile and whispered, "I need you," as quietly as possible. I knew she would be able to hear me. She gave a small, almost imperceptible nod and patted Mom's leg.

"I'll be right back, Mrs. Sullivan. I need to use the restroom."

I slipped back out into the hall before my mom could see me and waited for her.

"What's going on?" She sounded halfway between hopeful and worried.

"You're not going to believe this. Follow me."

"Believe what?"

"Don't ask. Just follow me," I said and led her back to the morgue.

Clarisse barely gave my father a glance as we entered. Caelyn was lying back on the cold metal table completely unmoving. She looked dead again.

"Connor. I already said goodbye…"

Cae's eyes opened and she let out a little, "Boo!"

"Well, shit," Clarisse said deadpan.

"What do we do now?" I couldn't help but ask her. She had *far* more experience than I did in situations like this. At least I hope she did.

"How did you do it?"

"Me? I didn't. I was all bawling and crying over her dead body when she woke up. I've done a lot of stupid things in my life, but turning my sister into a vampire isn't one of them," I replied, kind of hurt.

"We'll figure out the how later, though that bothers me more than what to do next."

"So you have a plan?"

"I *always* have a plan, worm. Wait here. I'm going out to my car to get an orb. We need to make her look human so we can get her out of here. Plus we don't want her going up like a match when we get her out into the sunlight."

"Yeah. That would be bad," my sister added from the table.

16

"You. Get out of bed and get dressed," Clarisse told her. "I'll find you something to wear."

"But, Mom, I don't wanna…"

"Connor. Go get your Mom. Bring her to your Dad and tell her to wait there. Good job with the mind trick, by the way."

Shit had just gotten serious. Clarisse *never* paid me compliments. I didn't make a big deal out of it and did as she asked while she went to her car.

By the time I got Mom and Dad situated in the hall and went back into the morgue, Clarisse returned with a glass orb in her hand and hospital scrubs under her arm. Without even a demonstration, she touched the orb to my sister's wrist. It melted and reformed into a thick gold bracelet. I turned around so she could get dressed.

"So. Are you like him?" Caelyn's question caught Clarisse a little off-guard.

"No. He's like me," she said after a moment of thought. I smiled at her response.

"She's dressed," Clarisse said.

I turned around and watched the orb worked its magic on my sister. Color returned to her skin visible outside of the hospital scrubs Clarisse had stolen for her, her talons were replaced by her normal fingernails, and her fangs disappeared completely. I gave a little sigh of relief. So did my sister.

"Go get your parents, Connor. We'll start with them."

I nodded and opened the door. "Mom, Dad, Caelyn is fine. Come on in."

"Oh, thank God!" They replied in unison and rushed into the room. I expected more drama and *way* more questions.

"How are you feeling, baby?" Mom wrapped her arms around her as she asked. "You gave us such a scare."

"Um… I'm fine?"

"Good. Now no more parties for you, missy. And consider yourself grounded for the next millennium!" Dad sounded angry, yet relieved.

Cae mouthed the letters, "WTF," over Mom's shoulder, begging me to explain.

I winked at her but shot a questioning look at Clarisse, who whispered, "I stopped in the hall and did a little mind magic of my own before I came in."

I nodded and whispered, "Thank you," back.

"Well, you guys head on home. I'll find Caelyn's doctor and thank him for fixing her up and all that," Clarisse said cryptically.

Mom and Dad's eyes glazed over once again and I felt the magic in Clarisse's voice. Caelyn must have felt it, too. She gave a little giggle and took Mom and Dad by the hand and herded them toward the door. Hopefully this would be the last trip we would ever have to take to the city morgue.

Chapter 2

My eyes opened. I screamed and slid up against the backboard of my bed. My sister perched at my feet like some sort of evil gargoyle.

"Jesus, Cae... Are you trying to give me a heart attack?"

"No. I'm bored."

"Go back to bed. What time is it?"

"Five in the morning."

"You do know it's Saturday, right?"

She nodded. "Yeah, but I've been up all night."

I gave a quick glance at her wrist. Sure enough, the gold bracelet was missing. "Where's your orb?"

"I took it off before going to bed. I wanted to check out my vampy self and I didn't put it back on. Why?"

"Well gee, Einstein. You're a vampire without it. Don't you think that might be why you're having trouble sleeping? At night? Being all nocturnal and stuff?"

I could actually see the moment of realization process itself in her normally focused on fashion and cosmetics brain. "Oh."

"Yeah. Make sure it's on when you go to bed. That will severely screw with your sleeping schedule. Don't need you passing out in the middle of Algebra from sleep exhaustion."

"It's going to take a while, isn't it?"

"For what?"

Sean Hayden

"To get used to everything. To get used to being mostly dead. To get used to being a vampire."

I nodded and got off my bed. It only took a few steps until I wrapped her in a hug. It was as unnatural as needing blood to survive, but it was a Hallmark moment. She didn't cry, but she took the hug and even scrunched my arm in hers. "I'll help, kiddo. You know that."

I felt her nod against my chest. "So. Explanation time?"

"Might as well. I'll tell you what I know, but I'm warning you. It's not as much as I would like."

"I wouldn't expect more. The universe might blow up if your head was full of knowledge."

I laughed and let her go. "Come on. Let's go somewhere for this. That way I can use visual aids."

"Huh?"

"I can show you my wings and stuff."

"Ahhh. Gotcha. Cool."

"That way we won't wake Mom and Dad up, too."

"I'll go get dressed."

"I'll leave a note for them. Tell them we went for a jog or something."

"Yeah. I'm sure they'll believe that."

"We went for donuts. They'll believe that." Caelyn nodded her agreement. "Don't forget your orb. The sun should be up soon."

My scooter pulled into the clearing Clarisse and I used for training. It was difficult traversing the dirt road with Caelyn riding on the back, but I managed to do it without wrecking.

My headlight sputtered dead when I turned the key off, plunging us into darkness. My Fallen vision illuminated the grass and trees around us with a silvery glow, making the clearing look like it was midday with cloud cover. Night vision never ceased to amaze me.

"I can't see shit."

"Take your orb off."

"Oh. *Oh!*"

"Pretty cool, huh?"

"Definitely. Connor?"

"Yeah?"

"Sorry," she said weakly.

"For what?"

"Being a shit. That's all the apology you'll ever get, so don't expect more."

I smiled and ruffled her hair. "I'm sorry, too."

I walked over to the middle of the clearing and stood there facing Caelyn. I called my wings and they appeared with a soft *thwump* behind me. Caelyn's eyes opened in wide fascination.

"Can I touch them?"

I nodded. "Be careful though."

"Are they fragile?"

"No, ticklish as all hell."

It probably wasn't a good idea telling her that. She *was* Caelyn after all. I felt her run her finger along the bone and the webbing between them. She behaved but couldn't help mutter, "Cool."

"I thought so, too, the first time I saw them."

"So you can fly?"

I gave a quick beat of my wings and hovered in the air above her before slowly lowering myself to the ground. "Yep. You might be able to someday, too. When I made Brett, he wanted to be a very specific type of vampire. He would have been able to fly if he lived longer."

"What?"

"He wished to be the kind of vampire that grows in power the older they get."

"Not that part. The 'when I made Brett' part. What are you?"

I sighed. If anybody was responsible for my sister's death it would be me, and she didn't even know. I just hope she would forgive me. Stepping back from her, I called my true form. She backed up even farther as I grew to my full eight feet. I saw my hands turn blue, my nails grow into crimson colored talons, and my hair lengthened until it reached between my wings. When I spoke, there was an otherworldly resonance that sent visible shivers down my sister's spine. "I am a Fallen."

"You're… You're… You're…"

"Basically a demon. Although they don't like to be called that."

Caelyn nodded almost imperceptibly. Of the million and a half questions she *could* have asked, she started simply. "How?"

"Well, it all started with a candle…" I banished my true form and my wings and made myself as human as possible before sitting down in the middle of the field.

For the next hour, I told her my story. I told her how I had sold my soul for my fondest wish. I told her how I met Clarisse for the first time. I told her about everything. She sat quietly through my whole tale.

The sky began to lighten and Cae slipped the orb on her wrist, becoming human once again. "So you made the vampire that attacked us?"

"Yes. I'm sorry. Apparently my magic is a little stronger than your average Fallen. The magic is supposed to take days or weeks to change a person. Getting slammed with that much power either made him crazy or he was crazy to begin with. Either way, he can't hurt anyone again."

"I remember. I was half conscious when I saw you yank his soul–or whatever it was–out of his body. That was pretty cool."

"Not for him. When you break the rules I mentioned, the Fallen come down on you pretty hard. So no eating people," I said with a wink.

Caelyn shuddered at my joke. "So what do I do now?"

"As far as?"

"Being a vampire. Am I going to have to eat people?"

I laughed, but stopped short. Honestly… I had no idea. But I knew how to find out. "I'm going to call a support group in for you. I honestly don't know. I'd be guessing if I gave you advice and I don't want to screw you up any more than I already have."

"Connor."

"Yeah?"

"It's not your fault, you know. Me dying. So don't blame yourself. Yes, you did make a stupid wish, but your responsibility ends there. I can hear it in your voice. Don't. Feel. Bad. We'll get through this."

"Together?" I finished for her.

"Don't push your luck. You're my brother. That doesn't mean I have to like you," she said. I breathed a little better when she winked.

I pulled out my cellphone and dialed Elizabeth Keating. She and Jenny Warburn were two vampires, created by the Fallen, who went to high school with us. If anybody could help Caelyn adjust to her new self, they could. They'd been there and done that.

"Hello?" I could tell Elizabeth was still sleeping when she answered the phone.

"Sorry to wake you. I need your help."

"Connor? It's six-thirty in the morning. Call me back after noon."

"It's an emergency. I'll consider it a personal favor if you help me on this one."

There was a moment of silence before she started speaking. "When and where?"

"The mall in twenty minutes."

"It's not open yet."

"I know, just meet me at the main entrance and bring Jenny." I clicked the off button before she could start asking questions.

I motioned for Cae to get on my scooter. With as fast as it could go over the dirt road, we would probably be getting to the mall at the same time as the Vamp Duo. Hopefully they wouldn't have any objections to making it a trio.

Chapter 3

We pulled into the parking spot right next to Elizabeth's black Explorer–or Exploder as she called it. The doors opened and she and Jenny stepped outside into the chilly November morning.

"This had better be pretty damn important, Connor. I need my beauty sleep."

"Yeah, you do," Caelyn added. Now normally this would have come out as a sarcastic sentence with the sole intent of belittling the intended target. That was how my sister rolled. Today, however, her comment sounded halfhearted and…almost…joking.

"Caelyn?"

My sister nodded and left the talking to me. "It is, Elizabeth. I wouldn't have woken you up this early if it wasn't."

"What's going on?" Jenny decided to join in.

"Well, my sister… She um…"

"I'm a friggin' vampire," Caelyn finished for me.

"What? Connor! How the hell could you turn your sister into a vampire?" Elizabeth sounded angry. *Very* angry. Pissed even.

"I didn't."

"I didn't mean you specifically. I meant how could you let *your kind* turn her into a vampire?"

"They didn't," Caelyn clarified. "I got bit. Drained actually. And I bit the vampire who did it to me…"

"A vamp can't turn you. That's not how it works," Jenny said.

"Forget what you know. Apparently, the ones I create can."

"Oh, great. I hope you stopped him from doing it again," Elizabeth replied.

I nodded. "Yeah. He um…won't be turning anybody again. Ever."

Elizabeth understood what I meant. She gave a small nod. "Okay. Good. How are you doing, Caelyn?"

"Still breathing. Sometimes."

"It takes a bit to get used to it, but you'll do fine. Come on. Let's go."

"Where?"

"My house for starters. Then the mall when it's actually open. Then lunch and more shopping."

"I um–"

"*You're* not invited. Girl-vamp day out. We'll get her transitioned. You know. You might want to let your people know that this is a good idea. I wish I had someone who would have helped me figure this out. Thankfully Jenny wished the same damn thing a week after I did."

I looked at Jenny who nodded her agreement.

"I'll mention it. I had one. I don't think it's fair that you guys don't." I turned to my sister. "You okay?"

"Yeah. This should be fun. Tell the 'rents I'll be home later. Thanks, Connor. For explaining everything and finding someone to help me."

"What are brothers for?"

"Mostly annoying the shit out of."

I watched their SUV pull out of the parking lot and sat down on my scooter. Pulling out my cell, I looked at the time.

It was almost seven-thirty. Hospital visiting hours didn't start until nine. I wanted to see Jessie.

"Screw it," I said and started my engine. I could always mind magic my way into the hospital if I needed to.

I pulled out onto the street and made it about a half a mile when a shiny red Harley pulled up next to me. I glanced over at Clarisse in her full leathers and tight red shirt...and drove into the back of a Volkswagen.

I stared up at the sky while I listened to the rumbly sounds of a Harley slowing down and turning around. The closer it got the louder her laughter could be heard over the sounds of her engine.

"Nice shot, worm. Nice dent, too." She cut the engine and pointed at the back of the car I crashed into. There was a nice Connor-shaped indentation in the back. You could even see my face print on the back window. I was lucky I didn't break it.

"Ow," I said and stood up. My scooter was unsalvageable so I banished it into nothingness. "Great. How am I supposed to explain this one?"

"Explain what?"

"The damage to the car."

"You are so dumb. I swear. I don't know what I...um...what Jesse sees in you."

"Huh?" She had started to say something else, but for the life of me I couldn't figure it out.

"Fix. The. Car. Instead of calling one into being, tell that one to fix itself."

"How?"

She sighed and got off her bike. She moved me out of the way, not too gently, with a push of her hand. I stood back and watched as she turned to face the rear of the car. She ran her hand over the damaged areas and I heard the creak of metal and soft popping sounds as the car miraculously repaired itself.

"Cool."

Sean Hayden

She stopped and motioned me to finish. I moved forward and felt the remaining dent beneath my hand. "Now picture how it should look as you push some power into it."

I did what she said and felt the metal smoothing out. I closed my eyes to help myself concentrate. "I can feel it," I said proudly and opened my eyes when the smell of charred metal hit my nose.

"Nice…uh…job."

I looked at what I had done. The car was perfectly smooth, but glowing red as the paint bubbled and charred around the repair.

"Maybe I should do the rest."

"Good idea," I said and stood back to let her fix it.

"I don't know what happened, but when Darius made you a fallen…"

"What?"

"You have too much magic. Way too much."

"What does that mean?"

She turned as she finished. I glanced down at the car and seeing it whole once again, breathed a sigh of relief. At least my rates wouldn't go up before I even got insurance.

"It means that if I had turned Brett into a vampire, he wouldn't have had half the power he had. If I try to fix a car, it gets fixed instead of turned into slag. I'm surprised that scooter you call into existence doesn't travel through time."

I gulped and nodded. "I wish I could control it."

"Have you tried? When I told you to fix the car, did you let the power trickle into it or did you cram it in there like you were trying to burst it open?"

"I don't know. I don't think about it. It didn't feel like I was cramming anything, but I wasn't trying to control it either."

"Try again," she said and her hand morphed into a claw in front of my face. She raked it across the back of the

28

car, gouging four slashes that ripped open the metal like it was made out of crepe paper.

I nodded and held my hand out again, covering the beginning of the damage. This time I slowly moved my hand across the damage while concentrating on letting the power drip from my hand instead of pouring from it. It worked. For a few inches. Then my hand pushed through molten metal. The smell of burning paint and hair wasn't a pleasant combination.

She sighed. "Well, I guess that theory sucked."

"Big time," I said as I pulled my hand from the hole I made.

"You need help."

"Know any psychiatrists?"

"Very funny. You need to get this under control or there will be issues.

"What do you suggest?"

"We can ask the Triad."

"What's a Triad?"

"The Council of Fallen. We're heading there anyway."

"Excuse me?"

"You've been summoned. I was on my way to collect you when you ran into the back of the car," she replied absentmindedly as she fixed the Volkswagen again. "There," she said and hopped on her Harley. "Let's go. Hop on."

I nodded nervously and swallowed the panic rising in my throat. I wasn't afraid of getting on the bike. I wasn't afraid of getting into a wreck. I was afraid of sitting behind Clarisse. She had an awful lot of exposed skin…

"Hurry up. We're already late."

I swallowed the lump and grabbed her shoulders as I swung my leg over the Road King Classic. I felt it rumble to life as I sat down on the leather seat.

She twisted the handle and the bike propelled us down the road faster than I liked. "Slow down!"

"Just hold on. You'll be fine."

My hands slid off her shoulders and down her back. I gripped her hips in an effort to stay on. She throttled even more and my hands involuntarily slid around her waist onto her hard stomach. I pressed my face against her shoulder and tried very hard not to look at the road.

I swear I felt her sigh beneath me, but I was too scared to think about it for more than a moment.

"Hold on tighter. We're going for a *ride*."

I didn't like how she said *ride*.

I looked over her shoulder at the road ahead of us. There was a flash of green lighting that opened up a twenty foot hole in the pavement in front of us. I thought she might try to jump it, but she leaned forward as her front wheel dropped, plunging us down the hole.

We fell into darkness.

It opened up into a dimly lit green sky. We and the bike fell toward a city illuminated in purple fire. The bike dissipated and Clarisse twisted in my grip. "You better let go and call your wings or it's gonna hurt when we land."

I let her go and with a loud *thump* she disappeared above me, slowing her descent. I did the same.

She dove and passed me, leading the way.

We glided down and she headed toward the tallest spire above the city. I closed the distance between us and called out to her. "What is this place?"

"Shade City, the capital of the Fallen realms."

I nodded and gulped, falling back after having my question answered.

She pulled up and floated onto a balcony near the roof of the tower. I landed, somewhat less gracefully, next to her. Without a word, she walked into the dimly lit interior. With little else to do, I followed.

The walls were made of polished black stone with gold streaks that glinted in the eerie purple flames. The chamber was enormous with a huge dais set against one wall. It's only feature was a gold, intricate rail that separated it from the rest of the room, guarding the three chairs behind it. Clarisse moved to the center of the room. She motioned to me as I hesitated some ways away.

"Hurry up, worm," she hissed and it echoed throughout the room.

I did, since she asked in her usual eloquent manner. "What is this place?"

"The tribunal room. The Triad will be here shortly." She stood at attention with her hands clasped behind her back, nodding for me to do the same.

A bell rang through the room as three Fallen entered the dais. I recognized Darius, the leader of the Reapers and Seekers, immediately. I gave him a small smile that he did not return.

The other two were as different from Darius as I was from Clarisse. One was garbed in dark metal plates that had been molded into wicked looking armor. It was matte black and reflected absolutely nothing. Strapped to his back was a two-handed sword whose handle rose above his long, silver-haired head by a few more inches. I was surprised. The Fallen could call their swords into being at will. To strap one to one's back was kind of unnecessary.

The third also had long hair, but of the whitest white. He had no facial hair, nor was he old, but he radiated age and wisdom the way Clarisse radiated sexy. He was dressed in flowing robes and carried a gnarled staff of black wood.

They walked slowly and surely in front of their thrones before sitting as one.

"Who stands before us?" The robed one asked Clarisse.

"It is I, Clarisse of the Seekers, Lord Agravius. I bring forth the one you seek, Connor, also of the Seekers."

"That remains the question. Step forward, young man. It is you we wish to speak to."

I did as he asked, standing before Clarisse. "Hello," I said humbly, earning a poke in the back from Clarisse. "Greetings, Lord Agravius," I amended quickly. She rubbed my back, letting me know I had finally responded correctly.

"It has come to our understanding that your role of Seeker may have been…misplaced."

I waited. Apparently he was waiting for a response. I didn't know what he wanted me to say. "I caused a problem that was not easily rectified. In my role of Seeker, I imbued one of my charges with too much power. He ran amok, injuring and killing humans in his thirst for power. I apologize with all that I am, my lord. I did not know it would happen." The words flowed from my mouth sweeter than honey. The problem was I had no idea where they came from. It wasn't from *my* brain.

He turned to look at Darius, who nodded agreement.

"Apparently, we wrongly chose your calling. What do you feel you should be doing? Look into your heart, young one. What does it tell you?"

I did as he asked and drew a blank. I knew I couldn't be a Seeker any more. It was too dangerous. At least until I could control my power better. "I know not, my lord. I have Seeked and I have Reaped. They are all I know."

"Do you seek knowledge? Is that where your strength lies?"

One word popped into my head: *Algebra.* "No, my lord. Learning nor wisdom has ever been my strength. I seek to make the world better. I wish to protect." Again the words flowed of their own volition. Too bad public speaking wasn't a calling of the Fallen. I could get used to this.

"Then perhaps Reaper or Warrior would better suit your talents. What say you, brothers?" He turned to face the two Fallen seated to his right.

"It is true. He reaped a soul so embedded in its body that even I had difficulty pulling it from its mortal coil. I would be willing to take him in and guide him," Darius replied.

"I would have to test him before drawing him into my legion of warriors," the other replied.

"It is your choice. Would you taste his blade now?"

"I would," the enormous Fallen replied with a nod as he stood. I didn't like the sound of it.

"Oh shit," Clarisse whispered from behind me, not filling me with a warm and fuzzy feeling at all.

"What?" I turned and asked her.

"Fight!"

I spun and saw the downward arc of the giant's blade. Without thinking, my black blades appeared and crossed to stop me from being split into equal parts of Connor.

Instead of being impressed by my blocking ability, he swung his sword to the side and back again, trying to slash me in half just under my arms.

I wielded two swords. Since the attack was from the side, using both blades to block would have been impossible without turning my body. I knew instinctively that to open one side of my body with *no* protection would be inviting certain death. I also didn't have a rat's chance in a crazy cat lady's house of blocking his massive sword with just one of mine. My body took over and, instead of blocking his attack, my blade met his and slowed it down, giving me the opportunity to jump back. As his blade swept past me, I closed the distance between us and brought both my blades down in a sweeping arc toward his thigh.

Just as my blades were about to connect, they disappeared.

"Enough, Lord Jun. What say you?"

"He would be welcome in our ranks," he replied and made his way back to his throne, not even breathing heavy. I, on the other hand, was shitting kittens.

Lord Agravius stood and walked down to the floor before us. "And what say you, young Fallen. Which is it you would prefer? Would you wish to rid your world of souls who have forsaken the rules set before them? Or would you prefer to be a warrior, should the need arise?"

I thought about it. Pros and cons flittered across my mind at flurrying speed. The thought of consistently pulling souls from humans rather turned my stomach. The thought of weapons training, strategy, and fighting also made me a little sick. I didn't want to do either.

I opened my mouth to tell him so, but that is not what came out. "I wish to join Darius. I know not if I could dedicate myself to the warrior's life. Perhaps in time, but not at this moment."

He nodded as if expecting my answer.

"So shall it be. Darius, he is yours," he said and returned to his throne.

"My lord," Clarisse spoke from behind me, "we have another issue at hand. I seek your counsel for a solution."

"What is it, child?"

"Connor has an unwieldy amount of power. He cannot seem to control it. It became apparent when his duties as a Seeker caused problems. There have been a few other instances, but none so clear as today. He caused damage to a human's property and tried to use his power to repair the damage. The first time he tried caused the metal to burn. I recommended trying to control the amount of power he was using, and he did. However, he was unsuccessful and caused further damage to the property."

"I see. Apparently I resumed my seat too early," he replied and stood once again, crossing the distance behind us. "Hold out your hand, young Fallen," he said when he once again stood before me.

I did as he asked and he grasped my hand in both of his. I could feel his power silently radiating off of him. "What should I do, my lord?"

"Pretend that I am the Volkswagen you inadvertently damaged while gazing at the flesh of young Clarisse."

I coughed in embarrassment, not really wanting Clarisse to know that particular piece of information. "I um…"

"Don't be silly, youngest one. If she did not want you to stare, she would not dress as she does. She does so for your embarrassment as well as your enjoyment, even though she would never admit it. Now. Pretend that I am damaged. Smooth out my damaged metal."

I did as he asked. I pictured the crinkled metal and let my power trickle out, smoothing it as it once was. There was a sizzle of burning flesh, the smell of smoke, and a sharp intake of breath as Lord Agravius quickly let go of my hand. "I see your point, Clarisse. Take the youngling back to his native world. You will continue with his instruction to the best of your ability. I will send…reinforcements." He turned and looked back at the dais. "Good luck with your new charge, Lord Darius," he said and strode from the room.

Sean Hayden

Chapter 4

We fell from the sky above our training clearing. There were no humans about to witness us, so we had no reason to hide. We flew in lazy circles and finally landed in the soft grass.

I didn't know what to say to Clarisse. I was still embarrassed from the comments the wizened Fallen had made about Clarisse's outfit and my enjoyment of it. She spared me from having to think of something to say. She opted for making things worse.

"Did you really crash your scooter because you were checking out my boobs?"

I could feel the heat creeping up my face from the vicinity of my neck. I couldn't believe she said that. "Er... Um. Shut up. You wore that on purpose."

She started laughing and the sound filled the clearing. "Maybe. You ready to train?"

"For what?"

"Well, I can't train you to Reap, so weapons practice or controlling your powers?"

"What time is it?"

She glanced down at the thin metal band on her wrist. "Ten in the morning."

"Shit. I've got to go. I promised Jessie I would be there when she woke up!"

I tried to ignore the look of disappointment on Clarisse's face. "Okay," she said weakly. "I've got to get to work anyway. Find me tonight and we'll continue."

"You got it," I said and called my scooter back to reality.

I glanced over my shoulder as I pulled away and saw Clarisse still standing in the middle of the clearing obviously lost in thought. The idea of that kind of scared me. I briefly wondered what she could possibly be thinking about as my tire briefly skidded in the dirt. I quickly regained control and forgot about Clarisse, eager to see Jessie as soon as possible without wrecking again.

Thankfully, visiting hours were open and I didn't have to mind magic the nurse to get to see my girlfriend. I peeked around the doorframe to see if Mr. James was in the room. Letting out a sigh of relief, I didn't see him in his usual position in the ugly green plastic chair by her bed. He might not hate me anymore, but he was still a big bad scary Chosen. Being mortal enemies put a serious damper on our relationship.

"Hey, beautiful," I said and entered her private hospital room.

"Hey, yourself," she said with a smile and *looked* at me.

Jessie was Nephalim, or one of the Cursed. Her mother was human and her father was one of the Chosen. A Nephalim's life was always riddled with misfortune until they became either one of the Chosen or died. It worked the same for the offspring of a Fallen and a human, too.

One of Jessie's many misfortunes was that she had been blind for almost five years. When her body healed itself, it also restored her sight. Neither her father, nor I, knew why she had been made whole again. I was just thankful she could see. She'd had her sight back for all of twenty-four hours and she had yet to run away screaming from me.

I crossed the room rather quickly and pulled her into my arms. I didn't kiss her, but I held her as close as I could without crushing her. "I missed you," I whispered.

"It hasn't been that long." She giggled.

"But it felt like forever."

"I love you, too," she said and pulled back, kissing me fully on the lips. "Sorry if I have morning hospital breath."

"You could have 'just ate a liverwurst sandwich' breath and I would still want to kiss you."

"That may be the sweetest thing anybody has ever said to me." Her giggle turned into fits of laughter. The sweet sound filled the room and made me smile. "Connor… We need to talk."

Oh shit. The smile left my face and I'm sure a great deal of color did, too. "About?"

"What happened last night. My father filled me in. Mostly. In a very cryptic way. Connor… I… I saw things. I saw you. What the hell is going on?"

I opened my mouth to tell her everything, but something stopped me. Although she still looked human, she might be changing into one of the Chosen. It was a distinct and probable conclusion. If she were, it wasn't my place to tell her. It was her father's. He and I needed to have a talk. Soon.

"That garage was completely full of paint fumes. It's no wonder you were hallucinating. Don't worry. I'm sure it will all come back to you."

She gave me a disbelieving look and shrugged her shoulders. "Well. Thank you for saving me anyway."

I kissed her forehead and gave me a quick smile. "So when you getting out of here?"

"Dad says sometime today. I'm fine, but they want to keep an eye on me."

I nodded. "Speaking of your father, where is the evil one?"

"Right behind you," came Mr. James' retort.

I closed my eyes and shook my head. "Did I say evil? I meant sneaky," I said to a wide-eyed Jessica, who broke out in even more fits of laughter.

"Hi, Daddy. Did you bring me Starbucks?"

"Venti caramel macchiato with almond milk and an extra shot, as ordered. How are you feeling, baby? Good morning Conrad," he said and put his hand on my shoulder as he leaned over and handed Jessie her coffee.

"Good morning, sir."

"What were you talking about?"

"I asked Connor what happened last night."

"And what, pray tell, was his theory?" He shifted uncomfortably.

"That the amount of paint fumes in that weirdo's garage was making me hallucinate."

He stroked his chin and seemed to think about it before nodding approvingly. "That's probably what happened. I'm just glad we found you."

"And the police still haven't found the guy?" Jessie didn't sound overly concerned. I would have been if I thought the guy who kidnapped me was still out on the streets. She didn't know that his soul was tucked safely away in one of the Fallen's realms. I hoped they had him making license plates or something.

"No," came Mr. James inevitable reply. "I'm not even sure they're looking that hard. His house went up in flames. They're probably expecting him to be three states away. If he's smart, that's where he will be. I'd very much like to get my hands on that young man."

Jessie's eyes widened a little. Her father sounded furious, yet calm. He even sent a shiver down my spine.

"So when am I getting out of here?"

"One more checkup from the doctor and you're free to go. I ran into him at the nurse's station. He should be here momentarily. Conrad, would you excuse us? There are some things we need to discuss. Would you care to come over tonight for a celebration dinner?"

"I'd like that, sir. Thank you. I'll see you tonight, Jess. Get some rest," I said and stood.

"I will. I'll miss you."

"I'll miss you more." I walked toward the door.

"Um, Connor?"

I turned. "Yes?"

She glanced furtively at her father who rolled his eyes and looked up at the ceiling. She mouthed the words, "I love you."

I winked and did the same.

Sean Hayden

Chapter 5

My stomach started rumbling as I swung my leg over my scooter. I hadn't eaten anything in almost twenty-four hours. That was unheard of. I briefly got over the shock that I wasn't passed out on the ground moaning for hamburgers.

I pulled out my cell, checked the time, and weighed my options. It was almost noon. Unfortunately I had zero cash. I could eat at home or go home and scrounge some pretzel cash from the old folks. The thought of soft, warm, salty pretzels left little room for decision making. I should probably check up on Mom and Dad anyway.

The drive was quick and uneventful. I pulled into the driveway and practically ran into the house. "Mom, Dad, I'm hooome!"

"Where's your sister?" Mom peeked her head out from the kitchen.

"She's still a little weird about yesterday. She's venting at the mall with some friends."

"She's grounded!" I heard Dad's voice from the kitchen.

I had forgotten all about it. I walked through the living room into the kitchen. Dad was sitting at the round kitchenette table eating a sandwich while Mom was doing something on her laptop at the counter. I looked over at Dad and caught his eye. I hated doing it but… "You told her she had suffered enough and let her off last night."

"Oh, okay."

Mom lifted her head up in shock and I calmly said, "You remember, don't you Mom?"

"Yeah," she said and went back to work. I had a little bit of a sick feeling in my stomach. It was getting too easy to mind magic my 'rents. Then I realized something. I wasn't a selfish kid. If you gave most teens the power that I had, their rooms would be full of gaming gear and nacho machines. My parents had it easy. I would *never* even consider doing something like that. *Or would I?*

Briefly, images of a PS3 flittered through my mind.

Only to be replaced by the image of the stack of bills by my mother's laptop. I sighed heavily. My parents worked *very* hard to make ends meet. I could never do it. Not in a million years.

"I'm meeting a few friends at the mall for lunch. Do either of you amazing people have a few dollars you could lend this poor, starving child?"

Dad laughed and set down his sandwich. "I have some cash. You're lucky you're charming like your old man." He reached into his pants and pulled out a bill. I took it without looking at the denomination.

"Thanks, pops," I said and kissed the top of his head. "I'll be back later! Oh, before I forget, Jessie's coming home from the hospital today. Her father invited me for dinner so I'll be eating over there."

"Okay, honey. I want you home by nine and you're staying home tomorrow. Family dinner night."

I smiled and grumbled under my breath. I hated Sunday nights. Family dinner night usually consisted of something with dairy in it that I couldn't eat, and fighting with my sister. "Okay, Mom. No cheese on mine," I reminded her futilely.

"Since when don't you like cheese?"

"Mom. Lactose intolerant. Want me puking all over the place?"

"Oh. Right. I forgot."

I rolled my eyes and left.

The mall was unusually quiet for a Saturday afternoon. There wasn't even a line at Aunt Annie's Pretzels. I gave a little internal *woot woot,* and walked up to the register. The girl behind the counter was facing the other way, leaning against the register, and filing her finger nails. I decided to be polite and wait. When the wait bordered on ridiculous, I began tapping the counter. The cashier looked over her shoulder and gave me an evil grin.

"I was wondering how long it would take you to try to get my attention."

"Shannon?" My mouth hung open in utter shock. Shannon MacVie was the head of the cheerleaders at James Underwood High School. She was also Shanria of the Chosen. And a royal pain in my ass.

"The one and only," she replied and turned around. I must say, the uniforms at Aunt Annie's Pretzels aren't appealing in any way, shape, or form. After seeing it on Shannon, I was forced to reevaluate my opinion of them.

"What are you doing here?"

"I work here. Just started today. They're already talking about promoting me to assistant manager," she said and rolled her eyes.

"But what are you doing working *here.* Shouldn't you be working at a clothing store or something more…um…fashionable?"

"Well I'm glad you think so highly of me. As it turns out… You got me addicted to the little doughy concoctions here. Working here affords me one perk that clothing stores do not… Free pretzels."

I couldn't help it. The ridiculousness of the situation became too much to bear. I broke down laughing in the middle of the mall.

"What's so funny?" She put her hands on her hips and I could see fire smoldering in her eyes. I held up my hands apologetically, but I couldn't stop laughing.

"I'm not laughing at you," I managed to croak out somewhat comprehensibly. "You are one of the most beautiful girls at our school. You are the head cheerleader. You drive a sports car. You could have any job in the world...and you're working here. For free pretzels no less." By the time I finished my explanation, my laughter had died down to a small chuckle.

She still had her hands on her hips, but her back went rigid, though not in anger. Her eyes had gone wide and she had a bewildered look on her face. I expected her to want a further explanation, but her question shocked me. "You think I'm beautiful?"

I'm surprised my jaw didn't hit the counter in front of me. "Um... Of course I do? I'd have to be blind not to think so."

"You're not just saying this because we broke bread and are not mortal enemies anymore, right?"

I sighed in exasperation. "Shannon. I don't do things like that. I say what I feel. You might have issues, but you are completely beautiful."

"Issues?"

I groaned. Talking to women was difficult enough. Give them wings and a superiority complex and it was damn near impossible. "Chosen-type issues," I said and blew out the breath I had been holding while I counted to ten.

"Oh. Yeah. I guess I see your point," she said and smiled. "Welcome to Aunt Annie's Pretzels, what can I get for you today?" Her voice had taken on a sing-song quality that nearly brought back another round of giggle-fits.

Through clenched teeth I said, "Two salted, please."

"Would you care for anything to drink?"

"Coke. Medium."

She rang it up and I pulled the crumpled bill out of my pocket. She gently pushed it away and hit a button on the register. The sale disappeared from the screen in front of me. "I think there's some fresh ones coming out of the oven. Let me check."

She turned around and walked behind a partition wall behind the counter. I stood in total, complete, and utter shock. The Chosen had been the mortal enemies of the Fallen since the dawn of time. Maybe if the Fallen complimented them on their appearance once in a while… *Nah.*

Shannon came back out holding a paper bag that steamed with pretzelly goodness. My mouth started watering uncontrollably. I had never, in all my years of being addicted, had pretzels straight out of the oven. I fought the urge to jump up and down as she handed me the bag.

"Hang on, I'll grab your coke."

I didn't wait. I jammed my face in the bag, inhaled, and ripped a piece off with my teeth, burning my lips in the process. I didn't care. I was a Fallen, I would heal, and I had hot pretzels. I moaned as I chewed. Shannon laughed as she handed me my coke. "They're better when they're hot, aren't they?"

I nodded, bowed, and said, "I love you," as I turned to go sit on the bench across from the store. "Fank fou," I called over my shoulder.

I sat in bliss, not paying attention to my surroundings while I ate. By the time I finished and stood, I finally noticed Shannon still standing where I left her, her hand still in the position to hand me my coke. It was as if she had been frozen to the spot. I shrugged and decided to wander around the mall.

Inevitably, I ended up in front of Angelique's Closet, workplace of Clarisse. It was a lingerie store and the odds of me actually going in to talk to her were a few degrees colder than absolute zero. Instead, I did what any teenage boy slash demon would do. I made faces at her in the window. She looked up from folding an incredibly small pair of women's panties, saw me, and rolled her eyes. I did however catch a hint of a smile in the corner of her mouth. She could deny it all she wanted, but I amused her. She hollered something at the woman in the back and walked out of the store.

"What did you break this time?"

"Huh?"

"Usually when you come see me at work it's because you created some sort of super-vamp or broke something that you need my help fixing."

"Oh! No. Nothing this time. I was just walking around and I stopped by to say hi."

"Well, it's my lunch break. Come eat with me."

I burped the last remnants of my pretzel feast and made a little more room for food. "Sure."

We walked silently to the opposite end of the mall where the food court lay nestled next to the entrance to the movie theater. "Wow," I said.

"What?"

"Was just trying to remember the last time I went to the movies."

"I get off at six. Let's go," she said with a funny tone to her voice.

"I can't tonight. Jessie's dad invited me to dinner."

"Oh. Okay."

I glanced over at Clarisse and she seemed a little down about something. "Everything okay?"

"Yeah. Why wouldn't it be?"

"I don't know. Even this morning you seemed a little sad. Just wondering if there was anything I could do to help?"

She gave me a small smile and headed for the pizza place. "No. Just thinking about work."

"Which job?"

"Both actually. I've been trying to think of who the Triad is going to send to train you and then I have to work tomorrow at Angelique's. I really don't want to."

"So call in sick."

"Huh?"

"Call in sick. We'll go see a movie tomorrow."

She seemed thoughtful for a moment. "If I do, and you cancel on me or forget, I will hunt you down, rip off your legs, and beat you to death with them. Do you understand?"

I gulped. "Yes, ma'am."

"Good worm. You want your pasta?"

"Yeah. Here. I actually have some cash."

"Keep it. You can buy popcorn tomorrow."

"Deal."

She ordered and paid, and I grabbed our tray. She wandered to the back of the restaurant and claimed a booth out of the way. I sat the tray down and set her salad in front of her. I left the pasta on the tray and grabbed us some plastic silverware and napkins. "Here," I said and arranged them neatly around her salad like we were dining in a real restaurant.

"Um… Thanks."

"You're welcome. So what else is new?" I sat down and tore into my pasta. For mall food it was pretty good. It didn't hold a candle to hot pretzels, but it would keep me alive.

"Are you actually making small talk?"

"I guess so. You sure you're okay?"

"Yeah. Just glad the whole Brett ordeal is behind us and that Jessie is okay."

"You and me both. Let's just hope I don't screw anything up when I start Reaping."

"Think of it this way, what's the worst that could happen?"

"Don't even go there. I don't wanna find out."

"Good plan."

"Clarisse?"

"Yes?"

"It bothers me."

"What does?"

"The idea of ripping someone's soul from their body. I know they broke the rules… I just don't know if I can do it."

"You'll do fine. Trust me. Once you start doing it, you'll realize that they not only deserve it, but you will be protecting innocents. The people on the Reaper list are not nice."

I nodded and focused on my pasta, hoping she was right.

Chapter 6

I wandered around the rest of the mall after dropping Clarisse back off at work. She gave me a quick hug before dipping back inside. I smiled. I liked the new, more mellow Clarisse.

One can wander around the same mall only so many times before it becomes quite boring. The mall was a lot like high school. You had your cliques. You had your hangouts. And nothing *ever* changed. I sighed and decided to head home and take a shower before going to Jessie's. I almost made it out the door without anything happening. *Almost.*

As I was walking past Aunt Annie's, I caught movement out of the corner of my eye. I spun expecting an attack. It wasn't too far from the truth either. A blond streak caught me in its arms and carried me across the entrance to one of the alcoves off to the side. I raised my arms to defend myself when I felt a set of very soft lips press themselves against mine. Arms wrapped around my back, pulling me in closer. My eyes closed involuntarily as I found myself being drawn into the kiss.

Clarisse had kissed me before. A couple of times actually. I couldn't believe she was doing it again. In the middle of the mall. In front of everybody. If Jessie found out... *Jessie!*

I mustered all the willpower I had and slowly pushed Clarisse off of me as she continued her assault on my mouth. I leaned in for one last peck, opened my eyes and said, "Clari–Shannon?"

Still in her uniform and smelling of warm pretzels, she stood there, still leaning toward me with her eyes closed. "Wow. Yeah. I've got to get back to work now. Thanks, Connor."

She opened her eyes and gave me a smile that belonged on a demon, not an angel. She turned and left while I stood there, watching her walk the whole way back to Annie's. I tried to tell myself it was to make sure I wouldn't get attacked again, but deep down I wasn't so sure. Not even a little bit.

I sniffed my pits one last time to make sure I put deodorant on and rang Jessie's doorbell. I waited the allotted thirty seconds it usually took for Mr. James to get to the front door, open it, and insult me.

"Evening, Conrad."

"Evening, Mr. James."

"Come on in. We're having ribs tonight. Jessie's favorite. Do you like?"

"It's probably my favorite, too. That and steak."

"Steak next time then. Want a beer?"

"Um… No thank you?"

"Good answer. Jessie's *watching* TV in the living room." I'm usually pretty dense, but even I could hear the happiness in his voice when he said that. I smiled, too.

"It's going to be weird on Monday."

"What is?"

"Jessie, going to school and being able to see. I've gotten so used to helping her to every class… It's going to be different. I'm looking forward to seeing what she thinks of school now that she'll be able to see it."

"Don't worry, Conrad. She'll still need you."

"Mr. James, she's so amazing I don't think she ever needed me to begin with."

That earned me a smile. "There is something I do want to talk to you about before dinner." He paused and looked down the hall to make sure Jessie was still in the living room. Motioning me to move over to the fridge, he opened the door and started pulling out salads and sides. "The ribs are in the oven to keep warm. There are mitts next to the stove. Grab those for me, would you?"

"Sure."

He continued talking while I put the oven gloves on. "I need you to keep an eye on her for me while she is at school. You know how being one of the Cursed works. She should have started transforming right away, yet she still appears to be human. If you see her changing...get her away from everyone else and call me. You can tell her whatever you need to. I don't care. Keep her calm and let her know what's happening. Can you do that for me?"

"Of course. You're not going to warn her in advance?"

He sighed and sat down on one of the barstools on the other side of the kitchen island. "Trust me, I thought about it. I wanted to. But… She is my little girl. I want her to have a normal life as long as possible. Now that she can see, she might even start enjoying it a bit more. Since we moved back to Cedar Hills, you've been the highlight of her existence."

"That's sad," slipped out of my mouth before I could stop myself.

"Conrad. Don't sell yourself short. For a Fallen, you're a pretty impressive kid."

"Yeah, well I'm still learning and screwing things up."

"Excuse me?"

And then it dawned on me. Shannon and the other Chosen at the school knew I wasn't really a Fallen. That I had been born human. Mr. James didn't. I didn't know whether to tell him or not. I was saved by Jessie coming into the kitchen.

"I thought I heard your voice. You'd rather hang out with my dad than me, huh? I see how it is."

Her joke, while it couldn't be farther from the truth, made me smile.

"I roped him into helping me with dinner. Plus, I wanted to thank him once again. I offered to buy him a car, but he refused."

"Daddy!"

He chuckled and started putting dishes on the table. I used his momentary lapse in observation to sneak in a Jessie hug. She took it one step further and kissed my neck.

"Knock it off, you two, and come and eat."

"Don't have to tell me twice. Ribs!" Jessie squealed like a little girl and ran to the table, leaving me with a Jessie-shaped hole in my arms.

I joined them and sat next to my girlfriend, keeping her between me and her father. He had mellowed, but I was still dating his daughter. He could turn on me at any moment.

We ate, mostly in silence. There was the occasional question from Mr. James that was responded to either by Jessie or myself. It came out as mostly grunts since both of us usually had mouthfuls of rib meat. We talked about school, homework, and anything else he could think of to keep the conversation going. I was happy just sitting with Jessie. Occasionally, I would make sure my fingers were free of barbeque sauce, and reach over to touch her leg or her arm. Every time I did it, I was given a small smile and blush.

When we finished, I offered to help with the dishes and ushered Jessie back to the living room. I really wanted her to take it easy. Mostly, I wanted to see if Mr. James wanted to ask me anything else.

He didn't wait long. "What did you mean that you were pretty new at being a Fallen?"

"Up until a few weeks ago, I was human."

"Excuse me?"

"I'm sorry, sir. I thought you knew. The Chosen at my school knew, so I assumed you did, too."

"Know what?"

"Clarisse."

"I'm confused. What about her?"

"I was doing my algebra homework and cut myself, when all of a sudden I got this *crazy* notion to make a promise in my own blood…"

"You wished to be a Fallen?" I could see the disgust on his face.

"Not my crowning achievement, but yes. When Clarisse showed up to grant my wish, I panicked. I didn't want *anybody* to have my soul when I was done with it. I thought I outsmarted them by wishing to become one of them… Now I'm not so sure."

"You dove headfirst into a world you knew nothing about. While you are correct it was not your crowning achievement, it was *very* brave."

"That's me. Stupid but brave."

"I'm not entirely convinced it was stupid either. You could have chosen worse. You could have ended up one of those sparkly creatures."

I laughed at his joke.

"Are you two done in there yet?" Jessie's voice could be very loud when she wanted it to be.

"Go watch TV with Jess. I'll finish up in here."

"Thank you, sir."

I made my way into the living room and sat down on the big brown-leather sofa next to Jess. She turned sideways, put her head in my lap, and stretched out across the rest of the couch. "What if your dad comes in?"

"He won't. I warned him that I was in *desperate* need of boyfriend snuggles. I also promised to behave, so don't get any ideas," she said with a wink.

55

I sighed happily and sank back into the sofa, enjoying the closeness. I began lazily stroking her hair and then her shoulder. I could tell she was getting sleepy just as I could tell she was fighting it. "Are you tired?"

"No."

"Good. Because I missed you."

"I missed you, too. What are we doing tomorrow?"

"I promised Claire we'd do a movie, but I'm yours the rest of the day." I felt her stiffen a little upon mentioning the movie. Jessie still had Claire slash Clarisse issues. I didn't like her being jealous. Not when she was my entire world. "Would you like to have dinner with me and my family tomorrow?"

She relaxed a bit. "If Daddy will let me out of the house." She sat up for a moment. "Dad! Can I have dinner at Connor's tomorrow?" Her voice was still reverberating through my head when he said okay. "Yes," she said simply and lay back down. I resumed my shoulder strokes.

"Jess?"

"Mmmm. Yeah?"

"You know–"

"If you mention Claire and how she's only a friend, I'll punch you. I know. It doesn't mean it doesn't get my panties in a bunch, but I know. I should probably rest up before going over to your house anyway."

Chapter 7

"Connor! Claire is here!"

Mom's voice echoed up the stairs and into my room. I glanced over at the clock next to my bed. It wasn't even noon yet. The movie didn't start until one. She was way early. "Coming!"

I jumped off my bed, shut off my Playstation, and dug through my dresser for a clean shirt to put on. Luckily I hadn't spilled any barbeque sauce on the jeans I wore last night. I had slept in them, too. At least I was partially dressed. I turned to head into the bedroom when Clarisse walked into my room. I let out a little *eep*, which she found highly amusing.

"Your mom said you've been up forever and were dressed."

"Yeah, well Mom was wrong."

"So get ready."

I sighed and opened up my shirt to put my arms through it when Clarisse gave a little hiss.

"What is it?"

"You're not going to be able to pass for a sophomore for much longer."

"What are you talking about? I am a sophomore."

"Have you looked at yourself lately?"

"Huh?"

"Bathroom," was all she cryptically said.

I headed there with her right behind me. I flipped on the switch, looked at myself in the mirror, and then at her like she had gone completely loony. "What?"

"Connor. *Look* at yourself. I turned and did it again. It was just me. Sure my hair was a little longer than usual, and a little lighter in color… "Oh, shit."

The change had been so gradual, I hadn't even noticed it. When you see yourself every day, you don't notice changes. Even drastic ones. My hair was a *lot* longer than it was only a few weeks ago. That wasn't the worst part. I thought it was getting lighter, but it was actually losing its color, bleaching itself almost white. I lowered my gaze to my shirtless chest. Gone was the little boy bird chest. I actually had pectoral muscles. My skin, while pale, was nearly flawless. The only thing that was *somewhat* normal, was the utter lack of chest hair. It made me look a little younger. Maybe the Fallen didn't grow chest hair. That would be nice since my father looked like he was wearing a bear pelt when he took his shirt off. He even had back hair. Back hair I said. *Shudder.*

"Holy shit," I said again.

"Exactly," Clarisse said and ran her finger over my left pectoral.

"Stop it!" I slapped her hand away and she giggled.

"Don't blame me. My little Fallen is growing up. Do you have hair in funny places yet?"

"Oh, my God. Would you please stop?" My face felt like it was on fire. She was enjoying this a little too much. "What the hell am I going to do? I can't believe nobody has noticed yet."

"Maybe they have and are just chalking it up to puberty."

My face went from "on fire" to "blazing inferno."

"No."

"No what?"

"No. Not ever. You don't get to use that word. Never."

She laughed and left the bathroom. "Put your shirt on and let's go. I'm hungry.

"You're always hungry."

"Being evil takes a lot of energy."

I laughed and put my shirt on, following her back downstairs. "Bye, Mom," I called out to the kitchen as we left through the front door.

Clarisse's pink Beetle was in the driveway, still running. We got in and she backed out, pointing us toward the mall. We drove in mostly silence until we pulled into the parking lot.

"How was dinner last night?"

"Nice. We had ribs."

"Nummy. Anything interesting happen?"

"Mr. James was uncharacteristically nice. That and he asked me to keep an eye on Jessie at school. So far nothing, but he's not convinced she won't suddenly sprout wings and a halo."

"Most fathers feel that way about their daughters."

"No. He thinks she might turn into a Chosen anytime now."

"I know, dork. I was making a joke."

"Sorry. Not used to that."

That earned me a punch in the arm as she pulled into a parking spot and killed the engine. We exited and started walking toward the food court entrance. "Anything else?"

"No. Not really. Jessie asked me to do something today and got a little jealous when I told her I was going to the movies with you."

She stopped a little short. "She's still worried about us, huh?"

"Yeah. She knows deep down in her heart that we're just friends, but she still gets a little growly when we're together. I've told her a million times I don't feel that way about you."

She gave me a strange look and started walking again. "Yeah. Like I could ever be into worms."

"I think I told her that, too. Although I said it a little differently."

"Ha. I'm sure you did. How did you say it?"

I pulled open the door and held it open for Clarisse, letting the warmer mall-air wash over us. "I think I said that you were way out of my league."

She stopped midstride. "Don't ever think that, Connor. You're a pretty amazing person." Shaking off the warm and fuzzy moment, she walked through the door.

"Thanks," I said and followed her inside.

"I'm sick of salad. What do you want to eat?"

"Anything but a pretzel. How about burgers?"

"Sounds good to me. What's with the sudden aversion to pretzels? I thought they were the main staple of your diet."

"They were until Shannon started working there…"

"Shanria Shannon?"

I nodded. "Yeah. She freaked me out yesterday."

Clarisse spun on me and looked angrier than I had seen her in a long time. "Did she hurt you? If she did, I swear I will send her back to her own plane with my sword!"

The other patrons of the food court stopped, glanced at angry Clarisse, and sidled away, seeking other restaurants to dine at. "Er... No. She didn't attack me. With a weapon. More like with her lips."

"What?"

"Yeah. As I said, it was weird. One minute she's giving me free food, warm ones right out of the oven even, and then as I'm leaving, she comes flying across the mall, carries me to one of the alcoves by the exit, and locks lips with me. I thought she hated the Fallen and me in particular."

"So did I. That is…most unsettling. Stay away from her."

"Planning on it."

"Good. Make sure you do."

"I will."

"Then I'll let you live." She turned and walked up to the register. The girl behind the counter looked like she wanted to run away. I didn't blame her. I did, too. "Double hamburger with pickles and mayo, large fries, make that two large fries, and a coke. And whatever Mr. Casanova Rico Suave wants. Girls like to give him free food." She moved to the side and gestured for me to order.

I tried very hard not to *look* embarrassed which was a far cry from how I was feeling at that exact moment. I kind of wanted to crawl into a hole and die. "Yes, I'll have the double embarrassment burger with no cheese, a large my-friend-is-a-psycho fries, and a medium Coke."

The girl lost it. She started laughing as she punched in my order, took one look at Clarisse's face, paled, and said, "That will be $17.93."

Clarisse handed the girl a twenty and walked off to find a table, leaving me to wait for the food. The girl handed me the change and gave me a small smile.

"Thanks," I said.

"Jealous girlfriend, huh?"

"How did you know?" I was a little perplexed.

"You can see it in her face. She's not too happy with you at the moment," she said as she nodded toward Clarisse.

"Oh. No. The jealous girlfriend is at home. She's just my friend who got angry because another girl kissed me yesterday."

I suddenly realized I probably said too much. The girl gave me a disgusted look and turned to get our food. I just hoped she didn't spit in it. "Here you go, Rico." She set the tray down and walked away.

Her attitude made me realize two things. One, I felt like shit because I understood how Jessie felt. Yes, Clarisse and I were friends, but if Jessie went to the movies with anybody else who just happened to have a penis, I would probably be grumbly, too. I owed her a big apology tonight and maybe more of an explanation. The second thing I realized was that the universe sucked. It totally wasn't my fault that Shannon kissed me and yet I still felt bad because it happened.

I picked up our food and wandered over to the table. I set Clarisse's food in front of her and kept mine on the tray. I sat down with a sigh.

"What's the matter with you?"

"Just thinking how unfair life is sometimes. I mean here I was, just trying to leave the mall, and a girl runs up to me and kisses me. Now you're mad at me, the girl that works at the Burger Shack is pissed at me, and if Jessie ever found out I wouldn't give you a nickel on my chances of survival. Hell, the bigger bet would be on who would kill me first, her or her father."

"Connor, I'm sorry. I had no reason to get upset with you. I apologize."

"What?"

"I'm not repeating it, so eat your embarrassment burger and shut up."

I laughed. "Thanks. That helped."

"No. Seriously. Hurry. The movie starts in twenty."

An hour into the movie, Clarisse put her hand on my knee. I tried to chalk it up to us finishing the popcorn and Clarisse needing something to wipe the butter off of her hand on, but I wasn't so sure. I didn't want to cause a scene by picking up her hand and moving it off my leg, either. It would definitely cause an all-out battle in the middle of the theater. I did the only thing I could do; I ignored it.

I didn't get to pick the movie. We were in the middle of some supernatural thriller about demons and angels. Clarisse had laughed through the first half, but we had gotten to a particularly steamy part of the movie involving the main character, an ex-priest who had been caught in an affair, and twin demon girls, whom he had no idea were actually winged succubae. I tried to chalk it up to the sex scene when Clarisse started rubbing my leg and moving a little closer to me. Her hand was getting harder to ignore.

"Um, Clarisse…"

"What?"

"Hand…"

She looked down and back up at me. "Oops. Sorry," she said but didn't move it, just stopped rubbing. I was half-grateful.

By the time the movie was over, I was sweaty and so ready to go that I felt sick. I silently reminded myself never to go to the movies with Clarisse again. Ever. I swear she enjoyed making me suffer.

"Well, that was better than I thought it was going to be. The demon twins were pretty hot."

I did a double take. "You think women are attractive?"

"Some of them."

"Huh. Nice to know."

"Why? You planning on meeting any succubae?"

"No. I think I already know one."

I fought the urge to do a little dance when I saw Clarisse blush. "You suck."

"Just getting you back for the hand thing."

"Did it really bother you?"

"More than you know."

"Good. Don't kiss other girls. Ever."

"I won't," I said as we made our way to her car.

"Since I have your word, you don't need to tell Jessie about Shannon. Unless you want to."

"I actually thought about it long and hard… I think I'm going to. It wouldn't be fair to *not* tell her. While I wouldn't be lying, it wouldn't be truthing either."

"You're growing up, worm. Don't say I didn't warn you when she punches you in the face, though."

"Wouldn't think of it."

"Uh oh."

Clarisse looked over at me from the driver's seat as we pulled up to my house. "What?"

"That's Jessie's dad's car. She's here already. I told her to come over at four. She's early."

"That's a bad thing?"

"I think it's more of an 'I want to inadvertently check on Connor coming home with his friend' type of thing."

"Ahhh. Gotcha. Want me to come in and pretend like you weren't all over me at the movies?"

"What!"

"Relax. I'm kidding. About the all over me thing any way. If you want, I will come in and act natural so she can see it's no big deal when we hang out."

"Do you think it would help?"

"Probably. Most likely. Shit, I don't know, but it couldn't hurt."

"Okay, then yes. Thank you."

"Just don't be a nervous ass when we get inside. Everything will be fine."

"Alright."

She parked on the road since the driveway was full of SUV. "Gosh, only sixteen and you're already having an affair," she whispered right before we got out of the car.

"Damn it, Clarisse," I hissed under my breath and opened my car door, wondering at the logic of letting Clarisse within five football fields of my girlfriend.

She giggled behind my back as we entered the front door. Everyone was seated in the living room. Jessie and her dad were sitting on our orange and yellow plaid couch, while Mom and Dad occupied the other two chairs. "Hi, everyone. Hi, Jess," I said and smiled at her. It wasn't forced either. Every time I saw her I got the goofiest grin on my face. She returned it until she saw Clarisse enter behind me.

"Hi, Mr. and Mrs. Sullivan. Hi, Jessica," Clarisse said.

"Hi, Claire!" My mom stood and gave her a hug. "Come on in and sit down."

"I need to get going anyway. Conrad can have my seat." Mr. James stood and patted me on the shoulder as he walked by me.

"Are you sure you don't want to stay for dinner?"

"Thank you, but no. I have some manuscripts that need editing. I just came by to drop the kiddo off. Enjoy your evening. Call me when you want me to pick you up, Angel."

"I will, Daddy."

"Don't be silly. We can bring her back for you," my dad chimed in.

"Thank you. I appreciate that. Nice seeing both of you again." He exited and I sat down next to Jess. Claire plopped down on the floor.

"Did you have fun at the movies?" Jessie's voice had a peculiar lilt to it, almost as if she was hopeful I didn't.

"It was okay. The movie was strange, but I didn't pick it out. Something with demons in it.

She laughed. "Rebirth of Onan?"

"Yeah. I think that was it."

"Yeah, not on my list of want-to-sees. When are you going to take me to a movie?"

"How about Friday?"

Sean Hayden

"Good. It's a date."

"So, how are you doing, Claire?" Mom started a conversation with Clarisse.

"Hanging in there. Going crazy between school and work. My mall job is gearing up for the holiday season. I've been going non-stop."

"Where do you work?" Dad made an effort to join the conversation.

"Angelique's Closet. It's a lingerie store in the mall."

"I know. I've been there a couple of times."

"Ewww, Dad. More than I needed to know," I said.

"What? I buy stuff for your mom for Christmas and birthdays. I'm allowed."

"Whew. I thought you were buying for yourself," I replied and gave him a wink. Clarisse and Jessie both started giggling. Mom just blushed.

"Er… Yeah. I'm going to start getting dinner ready. Honey, go start the grill. Claire, you're staying for dinner, too."

"Yes, Mrs. Sullivan."

"Jessie, would you prefer chicken or hamburger?"

"Chicken, please."

"Claire?"

"Both."

Mom nodded and headed toward the kitchen. Dad dutifully left to go start the grill. I took the opportunity to give Jess a quick kiss. "Missed you," I whispered.

"Did you?"

I frowned. "I always miss you when you're not with me. Don't ever wonder about that."

"I'm sorry. I'm being a brat, aren't I?"

"Clarisse, give us a sec would you?"

"Sure, I'll go help your mom in the kitchen."

I waited until she left the room and turned on the couch to face Jess. "Actually… No. No you're not. I had a bit of a realization at the mall today."

I saw the color drain from Jessie's face. I felt horrible. "What?"

"Not whatever you're thinking! Let me finish. I came to the realization that I was the one being stupid. I know you know that Claire and I are just friends and that's all we'll ever be, but… I thought about it. If the roles were reversed and you went to a movie with another guy, I'd probably be acting a bajillion times more jealous than you have. You've been really cool about Claire's and my friendship. So from the bottom of my heart, I'm sorry and thank you."

I watched as a single tear rolled down Jessie's cheek. I gave out a strangled *mrmph* as she tackled me on the couch and began giving me little kisses all over my face.

"No, Connor. Thank *you*. Thank you for putting yourself in my shoes and not being a stubborn dick. More importantly, thank you for *talking* to me about it. I love you!"

"Love you, too, beautiful."

Sean Hayden

Chapter 8

"Dear Monday, I hope you die," I whispered to the ceiling, hoping that something heard me. I didn't want to get out of bed. Not even a little. Mondays and homework should have their own constitutional amendment, banning them for all eternity.

"Are you up?" Mom stuck her head in my door. I resisted the urge to hurl a pillow at her.

"No. Can I be sick?"

"Only if you can fake blood coming out your ears. Get up, lazybutt."

I groaned and rolled over. "Five more minutes, Mom."

"Sweetie, it won't take me anywhere near five minutes to get a pitcher of ice water. You have two."

"You're evil."

"Now you know where your sister gets it from."

She left me to wallow in self-misery. When my internal clock registered a minute-and-a-half, I dragged the covers off my body. I didn't want to chance the pitcher of water that was more than likely on its way up the stairs. I passed Caelyn on the way to the bathroom. "How you doing?"

"Actually, much better. Hey. I need to thank you. For what you did and introducing me to Jenny and Elizabeth."

"What are brothers for? And don't say annoying the crap out of," I said and slipped into the bathroom, locking the door behind me.

Sean Hayden

It took me three minutes to get ready for school. Externally. Internally I was still nowhere near ready, nor would I probably ever be. I grabbed my backpack and headed downstairs.

"Hurry up, you're going to miss the bus," Mom said as I watched the big yellow cheese-wagon sail past our front window.

"Too late, I'll take my scooter. Want a ride, Cae?"

"Sure," she said and grabbed her backpack.

"I still don't like you riding that thing. It's dangerous."

"Yeah, well I don't have a job, so I can't afford a car."

"Connor, we discussed this. You may be sixteen now, but you're not ready to drive a car to school every day."

I sighed. "I know. The scooter is my idea of a compromise."

Dad came walking down the stairs. "I'd almost rather you drove a car. It would be safer than that little pile of crap on two wheels."

"Thanks, Dad!" I used his words against him and shot out the door making him think he had given me the green light on the vehicle. I was pretty sure Mom was inside reading him the riot act, and would be for quite a while. It might even carry over into that night's dinner conversation.

"That was pretty slick," Caelyn said as she joined me outside.

"Mom yelling?"

"You have no idea."

"Come on. Let's get going."

I spun the scooter around and let my sister hop on the back of the banana seat. Once she held on, I throttled out as fast as the tiny engine could push two people. We got it up to forty about three blocks down the road. "Slow down, Sir Speedy," my sister laughed in my ear.

"Shut it. It's better than yours."

"True."

"I'll make you a deal."

"What?"

"*If* Mom and Dad sort out the fight and I'm actually allowed to get a car, the scooter is yours if you want it."

"Hell yes! Thanks."

"Least I could do."

We pulled into the school parking lot and parked. We even walked into school together, which was even more unheard of. Maybe my sister getting turned into a bloodsucking creature of the undead wasn't a bad thing.

"You need a ride home?"

"No. I have cheerleading practice and then I'm meeting Elizabeth at her house. She's helping me with some homework."

"Okay. Be careful."

"Doing homework or splits?"

"Splits. There's some Chosen on your cheerleading squad. I don't know if they'll be able to see through your orb. They might not appreciate a vampire on their squad."

"Chosen?"

"Yeah. The Fallen are the good guys who look like demons. The Chosen are the angelic ones who are real assholes."

"Um… Okay. Who?"

"Shannon and her two lackeys."

Caelyn's eyes doubled in size. "I knew it!"

"What?"

"That she wasn't human. The bitch does like three thousand sit-ups a day."

I couldn't help it. I laughed. "Just watch your back. If you have any problems, let me know."

"Okay, big brother. Thanks" She disappeared down the hall toward her locker. I kept walking to find mine and hopefully Jessie.

I nodded to the few friends I saw. James Underwood High wasn't a large school at all. We had around two hundred kids per grade, making the entire school's population around eight-hundred including the teachers and staff. Everybody knew everybody, and everybody knew everybody's business. It was both charming and annoying.

I opened my locker and tossed my backpack inside, grabbing only the books I would need for the first two periods. English and Algebra, my favorite. I didn't mind English, but I still bore a grudge against Algebra for turning me into a demon. Yet another reason why homework should be outlawed. I should move to France. I heard they were outlawing homework.

I closed my locker and jumped. Jessie had been standing behind the door waiting to scare me. She succeeded. "Morning, sexy," she said and leaned in for a kiss.

"Morning, beautiful. How are you this fine, fine day?"

"Pretty damn good now that I'm not fumbling around the halls not being able to see."

"I imagine. And what do you think of the beauty that is our fine establishment of learning?"

"It's boring. I pictured way more color in my head. Maybe I'll just keep my eyes closed while I'm here. Except when I'm looking at you of course…"

"Good answer. And not a bad idea. I keep my eyes closed for most of the day here, too."

"That's because you're sleeping. Come on. Homeroom. We don't want to be late."

"You don't, I do," I said and took her arm out of habit.

"You know you don't have to lead me around anymore."

"Shhh. Close your eyes," I said and winked.

She snuggled closer, but kept her eyes open anyway. "Thanks."

"Anytime."

Homeroom was quick and English seemed to drag on forever. I expected Algebra to take twice as long to get through. At least we'd have lunch after two more periods and one of them was PE.

Everyone in class was surprised at Jessie walking around without her customary white cane. It had been the same in homeroom. And walking through the halls. And everywhere else we went. It was during a flurry of excited congratulatory hugs and praises that Jessie took her usual seat next to me as Mr. Johnson began his monotonous drone about exponents.

"I hate Algebra," I whispered under my breath.

"Yes, but at least you're better at it than everyone in the class."

I was a little surprised that Jessie could hear me. I had *barely* whispered it. "Yeah, now. I didn't used to be," I whispered again to see if she could hear.

"I can't imagine you being bad at anything."

"Who are you talking to Ms. James?" Mr. Johnson turned and stared directly at her. I was whispering. Jessie hadn't.

"Myself. Sometimes when I repeat things I have a better chance of remembering them," she lied smoothly.

"Well do it quietly, please."

He turned and went back to making slash marks across the green blackboard. "Nice one," I whispered.

"Thanks," she whispered back.

"I love you."

"I love you, too." She forgot to whisper. Everyone in the class started to giggle. Mr. Johnson didn't seem as amused.

"See me after class, Ms. James."

"Oooh," everyone chorused.

Jessie blushed and gave me a dirty look. I did my best to look apologetic. I hoped she didn't get into too much trouble. "Sorry," I whispered again.

"Shhh."

"Since you don't feel the need to pay attention in my class, why don't you come up here and solve for Y for me?" He held out his piece of chalk, not allowing her to back down from his challenge.

Jessie stood and walked to the board, taking it from him as she passed. She stared at the board briefly and let fly. Her arm was almost a blur as she wrote the complicated answer beneath the initial line. Mr. Johnson looked over at me, mouth agape. It would appear I wasn't the only algebra prodigy to spring up in his class…

Oh shit. I fought down the panic. A few weeks ago, I had done the exact same thing when my Fallen powers began to manifest. All of a sudden, I could see glowing numbers in the air in front of me. The problems began to solve themselves. All I had to do was copy them down. *That means she could be changing, or just got really good at math.*

I didn't know what to do. Solving for Y was hardly a reason to panic and call her father. I looked around the room. Everyone else was staring at Jess. Something white in the corner of my eye caught my attention. On her seat was a solitary white feather.

"Damn," I said and didn't whisper.

"She's good," someone else said.

I knew the change was coming. I didn't have enough solid proof to tell Mr. James; I *would* however, tell him the next time I saw him what had happened. Hopefully, the change wouldn't happen quickly. Hopefully, we had time. Hopefully, she would still love me when she found out what I was…

I slid into the lunch line right behind Jessie. "Hey beautiful, is this spot taken?"

"Why yes it is. By a handsome man who just happens to look like you."

"I'll kill him!"

"Dork. How was PE?"

"Cold. You're lucky you have study hall."

"I am."

"Sorry about before… How much trouble are you in? Johnson give you detention?"

"No. He lectured me and let me go. And it wasn't your fault. I'm the one who needs how to learn to whisper."

"Salad for the lady and sloppy-joes for me," I told the lady behind the counter.

"How do you know I didn't want sloppy-joes?" Jessie gave me a wink.

"Because you're smarter than I am? Duh. I thought you knew that."

"I think you're smarter than you give yourself credit for. I also think you need to quit putting yourself down every opportunity you get. It's one of the few things about you that drives me crazy."

"Gasp! You mean there's *more*?"

"Yes. You're way too attractive. I'm going to have to start beating the girls away from you with a stick."

I frowned at her statement. *If you only knew the half of it…*

I still needed to tell Jess about Shannon. I had meant to earlier, I just hadn't had the opportunity. At least that's what I kept telling myself. The truth was I didn't want to hurt her and I didn't want her to hurt me.

"What?" She looked at me quizzically.

"Come on. Let's eat. I'll tell you over lunch."

"I really don't like the sound of this…" She picked up her tray and walked over to our usual table. Clarisse and Jeremy, who normally ate with us, were thankfully absent. She put her tray on the table, sat down, and folded her hands over her food, waiting expectantly.

"Aren't you going to eat?"

"After. Maybe."

I gave her a half smile. "It happened Saturday…"

"*What* happened Saturday, Connor?"

Oh shit, she said my name. "I went to the mall to get some pretzels. Shannon got a job there and was working–"

"Shannon who?"

"Shannon. Cheerleader. Senior Shannon."

"Okay?"

"Well she was acting all weird. She gave me free pretzels, I said thank you, ate and left."

"That's it?"

"Well no, I haven't gotten to it yet."

"Talk. Now."

I gulped and took in a large breath. "Well, I walked around the mall for a bit and when I was leaving, she sort of ran up to me and kissed me."

Her face went blank. She calmly reached down and grabbed her salad dressing, opened it, and began pouring it over her salad. I expected her to say something, anything, but she just started munching on lettuce.

"Are you okay?"

"Yup, I'm fine."

"Aren't you going to say something?"

"Trust me, you don't want me to say anything right now. Eat."

I sighed, doubted my wisdom in saying anything, and tore into my sloppy-joe. We sat quietly for almost ten minutes before the silence was broken by Clarisse sitting down with a tray of food next to Jessie.

"I hate school. Have I mentioned that lately?"

"Did you know?" Jessie calmly sat her fork down and turned to look at Clarisse.

"Know what?"

"Connor just shared some interesting information with me."

Clarisse looked over at me. I looked down at my food. "About…"

"Don't play dumb, Claire."

I panicked. I was worried Clarisse would think I had told her about the movies. "I told her about Shannon," I said apologetically.

"Good," Clarisse said and started eating.

"Good? He kisses a girl and you say good?"

"Yes."

"Would you care to elaborate? How is it good that my boyfriend is kissing other girls?"

Clarisse sighed heavily and set her fork down. She turned to look Jess right in the eye. "First of all, yes. I knew all about it. Connor told me about it at the movies. I didn't tell you because he said he couldn't keep anything from you and it would kill him if it hurt you to find out what happened. I even told him not to tell you about it.

"Second of all, he didn't kiss her. She practically attacked him and kissed *him*. His first thought? To tell you about it. So think about it, Jessie. He didn't do it, he didn't want to do it, and he still told you about it. I'm not saying you shouldn't be mad. I'd be pissed, too, but you shouldn't be mad at Connor. You should be thanking him for telling you about it and not keeping things from you."

She turned and picked her fork up again and started eating. I had trouble believing she had stuck up for me as vehemently as she had. It sounded like she was expecting this conversation and had rehearsed her lines. They had come out that naturally.

I looked from Clarisse to Jess who stared at her salad like she would find some sort of wisdom hidden between the layers of leafy green goodness. "I'm sorry, Connor," she said and started eating, too.

I didn't want to say anything that could possibly have a negative impact on the situation. If she had been looking at me, I would have given her a smile. "I love you," I whispered. "I'm just sorry it happened at all. If it makes you feel any better, I will be avoiding both Aunt Annie's Pretzels and Shannon for the rest of my life."

Jessie looked up from her salad and opened her eyes as far as they could go. "You'd give up pretzels? For me? You really *do* love me," she said and grinned.

"More than pretzels."

"I'm not hungry anymore," Clarisse said disgustedly.

Jessie and I laughed and finished our lunches. We sat quietly until Claire finished hers and we stood to leave together. Life is kind of funny, sometimes. Just when you think things have gotten back on track and you might be heading toward some sort of normal, that's usually when the powers that be decide to derail your train.

As we were leaving, Shannon decided to make a grand entrance to the cafeteria with her two lackeys in tow. I groaned inwardly as soon as I saw her blond hair come through the doorway. *Please don't say anything, please don't say anything...*

Her gaze swept right over Jessie and Clarisse and settled upon me. Her pouty lips curved into a sultry upward smile and her eyes narrowed as she looked down at my shoes and all the way up to my face, meeting my eyes. "Hello, Connor... Long time no–"

The impact of Jessica's fist sent a clap of thunder that reverberated through the James Underwood High School cafeteria like a sonic boom. At least that's what it sounded like to my ears. It must have been pretty loud to everyone else, too, because everyone turned around to watch Shannon fly back between her friends and land, skidding, across the linoleum floor.

"Kiss him again and you won't wake up from the next one," Jess said as she walked passed her prone form.

I hurried to catch up to her and Clarisse, avoiding any sort of eye contact, physical contact, metaphysical contact, or anything that could be construed as any sort of contact with Shannon. I didn't want to be on the receiving end of one of those punches. Ever.

Sean Hayden

Chapter 9

"You okay?"

I turned and saw my sister as I was getting on my scooter. "Yeah, why?"

"Saw the fireworks at lunch. Just making sure you weren't on the receiving end of any of them."

I laughed. "No. Her rage was focused solely on Shannon."

"What the hell happened?"

"I'll tell you when you're a little older, kid."

"Fine. Then I'll tell Mom your girlfriend knocked out the head cheerleader at lunch today and you won't tell anyone why."

"I was just kidding. Sheesh. No need to resort to blackmail."

"There's always a need for blackmail when it gets me what I want."

"Evil bloodsucker."

"Evil Demon."

"Touché. It was actually kind of weird. I was at the mall and Shannon kissed me. I felt bad about keeping it from Jess, so I told her."

Cae shifted from foot to foot and looked like she wanted to say two million things to me. "Um…"

"What? Spill it."

"I'm having a little trouble believing that Shannon kissed *you*."

"Gee, thanks."

"I'm not saying anything about you... I...um... Okay. You didn't hear this from me, but I wasn't even totally sure that she liked..."

"Fallen Ones?"

"No."

"Younger men?"

"Closer."

"Dashingly handsome younger men?"

She rolled her eyes. "More like men in general. Let's just leave it at that."

Oh, how the gears in my head started turning. That was kind of *hot*. "Wow."

"You're daydreaming about it now aren't you?"

"Yep."

"Perv. Anyway. This is the point in our conversation where I get to tell you you're a dumbass."

"Why?"

"For telling Jessica. Do the words 'death wish' mean anything to you?"

"Okay, picture this. Shannon kisses me. I *don't* tell Jess about it. Jess finds out about it..." I let my words trail off for maximum effect.

"Good point. I guess there really is a fine line between dumbass and genius."

"And I cross it every day."

"Yes, but sometimes you regress."

"Can't help it. I'm a guy."

"Too true."

I laughed. "How you doing? Everything okay? You didn't drain anybody into a raisin-like husk at lunch, did you?"

"Okay, this is going to sound weird. Elizabeth and Jenny can drink animal blood."

"Too much information, but continue."

"Well, it turns out, I can't. I'm a different kind of vampire."

"Tell me you're not feeding on people…"

"People, no. Vampires, yes. Jenny cut her finger and before I knew it, I was latched on and feeding off her."

"Was she okay with that?"

"Um. Yeah. Apparently it feels good when I feed. Like *really* good."

"Re-entering the land of I-don't-need-to-know-this."

"That's not a real place."

"Sure it is. It's in Asia. Look it up."

Caelyn laughed. "You're a dork."

"And you're related to me. Bwahahaha."

"Don't remind me."

"So you're doing okay?"

"Yes. I'm fine. Thanks for worrying, though."

"Big brother duty, number twelve. You sure you don't want a ride home?"

"Nope. Going to Jenny's."

"Don't drain her dry."

"I won't," she said and turned to leave. I watched her go and gave a little smile. For the first time in a few days I had a feeling that she was going to be just fine.

I started up my engine and let it run for a few seconds before turning it around and heading out of the school parking lot. Clarisse honked as she passed me, turning the corner and almost getting the VW Bug up on two wheels. I shook my head. I liked Clarisse a lot, but I didn't miss riding in her car every day. I might be immortal, but riding with her was just tempting fate.

I felt my cell phone buzz in my jacket pocket. When I hit the first red light, I pulled it out. It was a text from Clarisse.

Clearing, twenty minutes. Don't be late. Company

I had no idea who she could be bringing, but I would find out soon. The clearing was only ten minutes away. I

Sean Hayden

would even pass Rockin' Robin's Convenience Mart on the way. I was still hungry and had time to pick up a snack.

I pulled into the clearing with half a Twinkie in my mouth and an Ice-nado cherry beverage precariously perched in my left hand. Driving a scooter, holding a beverage, and eating a snack-cake was damn near impossible, but I pulled it off without wrecking.

Clarisse wasn't there yet, so I parked and finished my food, feeling a little more human...or whatever I was. Two minutes later, she pulled in. She wasn't alone either. There was a passenger in her car, and it was difficult to make out any details with the sun's reflection almost blinding me off the windshield.

She pulled next to me and both doors opened as the engine shut off. Clarisse got out first and a woman with black hair soon followed. I gulped as she got out of the car. She wore black jeans and a black T-shirt. She even had black Converse high-tops on. *Wow.*

"Connor, this is your new instructor, Raven."

"Let me guess, because she wears all black?"

"No. Because she'll claw your eyes out if you do anything stupid. So quit talking," Clarisse answered.

The new girl didn't even smile. "Hello," I said and earned a nod from her.

"Raven is a Reaper like you. She'll teach you your duties and so forth. She also will be helping you try to control your magic."

"Okay... I thought you were helping me with that."

"Relax. I'm not going anywhere. I'm still your babysitter for the next century or so."

And it was at that moment that the true meaning of the word *immortal* sank in. I didn't have to worry about getting

84

married, finding a job, raising a family, retirement, 401(k)s, nursing homes, or adult diapers. I would be the way I was for centuries. Maybe even millennia, provided I didn't get myself killed to death. "Wow."

"What?"

"Century. Long time. Immortal moment."

"Welcome to what you wished for," Raven finally spoke.

Her voice sounded like someone had mixed black paint with smoke. She wasn't raspy, or even a baritone, it just held an edge of darkness tinged with something that would be very bad for you. She sounded dangerous.

I nodded my agreement. "Just kind of hit me all at once."

"I can imagine. You're very lucky, human."

"Alright. I'll leave you two to get to it."

"You're leaving?"

"Work. Remember? I wasn't kidding when I said they were gearing up for Christmas. Don't worry, Raven won't hurt you. Much."

"Okay. Have fun. Thanks," I said and tried to muster as much sarcasm into it as inhumanly possible. Clarisse shot me an evil grin, letting me know I had succeeded.

"Center of the field, now. Let's see what you've got."

I followed her out into the circle of grass that had been cut out of the surrounding trees. She held out both hands and motioned me to put mine in hers. I did as she asked and gasped at the coolness of her skin.

"What?"

"Your hands are cold."

"I am pulling with them."

"What does that mean?"

"I am told that you have already Reaped a soul. Is that true?"

"Yes."

"Remember how you pulled the soul from the body of the mortal?"

I nodded. "Yes."

"That is what I'm doing now."

I almost yanked my hands from her grip. "Stop!"

"Relax, young one. I cannot rip the soul from the body of a Fallen. None can. Our bodies are not vessels for souls. They are one. It is one of the sources of our powers."

"Oh. Okay," I said and relaxed a little.

"I am pulling so my body will absorb the magic that you throw off. That way there will be no...accidents."

"Ahhh. Gotcha."

"Now, push with your magic like you wished to do me harm."

"You can do that?"

"Yes. As long as you're touching your opponent, your magic can be quite damaging."

"Can't shoot it though, huh?"

"Pardon?"

"Shoot it. Like fire lightning bolts or magic missiles from your hands."

"Some can, but only the very strongest of us. The ones you would have considered archangels before the Rift."

"Damn. That would have been cool."

"More likely, dangerous."

I nodded and closed my eyes. I pulled the magic from inside me and hurled it with everything I had from the center of myself and outward through my arms. One second Raven was holding my hands and the next, she wasn't. I opened my eyes to see her sprawled out on the ground five feet away, rubbing her hands vigorously.

"Are you okay?"

"Yes. I wasn't expecting that, I will tell you." She stood and walked back to where I stood. "Again, but this time try and control it. You want me to feel it, but you don't want to cause damage."

I concentrated again and let the power trickle outward. Again, her hands flew from mine. Again, she was on the ground rubbing her hands against her pants. "I did it again?"

"Yes. But I noticed something."

"What?"

"The amount of power was still incredible, but it was a different sensation."

"And that means what?"

"I don't know, but we will find out. I have a theory."

"Oh good. Theories are good."

She nodded, not understanding my sarcasm. "Again, but I want you to try something different."

"What?"

"I want you to… I want you to imagine sticking my hand with the smallest of needles."

I nodded, closed my eyes and gave it another shot. She said nothing. I opened my eyes and saw her grimacing in pain, but holding on. I stopped pushing. "I guess your theory worked."

"It did. This time keep your eyes open. Do the same again, but picture more needles."

I did what she asked. Her face went from grimacing to contorting with pain. "Want me to stop?"

"No. Picture more needles. Longer ones."

I did *exactly* as she asked. Quickly, she gave a shout and let go. At least I didn't blast her away from me this time. "Did I do it right?"

"Yes. And we have the key to your control."

"Needles?"

"No. Intent."

"I don't understand."

"Your magic is too…raw, for lack of a better word. Instead of controlling the magic, control what you intend to do with it. For example, when you turned the boy into a vampire, instead of focusing on turning him into a vampire, you should have focused on telling his body to turn him into a vampire, *slowly.* Does that make sense?"

"Oddly enough, it does."

I thought about it, and instead of screwing the idea up, it actually began to make even *more* sense. "Give me a second, I want to try something," I said to her and walked over to my scooter. I raised my fist and punched the metal fender, putting a nice sized dent in it. The last time I had tried this, I left a molten hole. This time, instead of throwing my magic at it and telling it to fix itself, I ran my hand over the dent and slowly imagined tiny hammers making it whole once again. When I no longer felt the dent, I moved my hand. The paint was still messed up, but the fender was fixed, and more importantly, not melted.

"Better?"

I turned to Raven and nodded. "So far. Now I just have to fix the paint."

Again, I held my hand over the damage. This would be a little tougher. I imagined all the paint molecules letting go and doubling in size. As I felt it squirm beneath my hand, I imagined it hardening once again.

This time, when I moved my hand, you couldn't tell there had ever been any damage to the area. "Perfect," I said and turned around.

"Good." Raven nodded and called her blade into being. "Since that took less time than I expected, let's get some weapons training in.

I looked at her sword. Like mine it was matte black with reddish runes on it, but she had only the one. I nodded and called mine into being. The more I did it, the more the blades felt comfortable, *right*, in my hands. "I'm warning you…"

"Don't get cocky, I sincerely doubt you will best me."

"That's not what I was going to say. I was warning you that I suck and I'm nowhere near as good as Clarisse..."

"Oh. Then we will focus on weapons training as a part of your daily routine. You never know when the need to defend yourself will arise."

"Oh goody."

She seemed perplexed by my statement. Raven didn't get sarcasm at all. "You actually wish for combat?"

I sighed. "No. That was sarcasm."

"Ah, forgive me. It has been long since I have ventured to your realm."

"Don't get out much, huh?"

"To say the least. Your world is best left to the youngest of us."

"Like Clarisse."

"And you. And others. We elders tend to live solitary lives. I only came forth because I was asked."

"Because of your experience?"

"That and my power," she replied.

"You're...an archangel?" I didn't have a better word.

She nodded and I watched her eyes smolder with black fire. "We do not call ourselves that."

"What do you call yourselves then?"

"Damned," she replied sadly and I could almost feel the pain pour off her.

"Are things so bad?"

"If you knew what we *used* to be, what was taken from us, then you would know exactly how much we have lost."

I began walking toward her, readying my blades. "I'm young, and I'm not that bright, but it seems to me that all of you, the Chosen included, would be a lot happier if you stopped focusing on what you were and started worrying about what you could be."

Raven laughed, not unkindly either. "I think you should stop thinking of yourself as not that bright. To me, you seem a little wiser than your years should allow. Ready?"

And thus began the most tiring, rigorous, dangerous workout I could have imagined. She blocked my two blades with her one every time, without effort. Before I even began to *think* about moving, she was already there, knocking my blade aside and tapping me with her blade. She was utterly amazing. The sword seemed to be more a part of her than a weapon. I wanted to be just like her when I grew up.

"How can you be so fast?"

"It will come in time. You're actually at a disadvantage. You may have unbelievable raw power, but you're limiting your body by having been human. You only think you're moving as fast as you can. You could actually move a lot faster if you believed it."

"I only know what I'm used to. I don't know how to be different."

"I know. It is why I said it will come in time. The more you practice, the quicker you will learn how very much you can do."

She finally slapped both my blades from my hands with a well-placed attack of her own. They dissipated into nothingness before hitting the ground. "Wow," I said simply.

She nodded. "Enough for today."

"Thanks, Raven. You helped me a lot today."

"I will help you more tomorrow."

Chapter 10

I spent the rest of the week going to school, training with Raven, doing homework, and spending as much time as I could with Jess. By the time Friday rolled around, I was more than ready for the weekend. Thanksgiving was the following week, so it would be a short week at school. But for now I wanted nothing more than to relax and take Jess to a movie like I had promised.

Her dad would be dropping her off at the theater at eight. That left me two hours to train with Raven, get home, take a shower, and meet her there. I headed to the clearing right after school.

She was there, waiting in her usual spot, just like always. "Hi, Raven."

"Greetings again, young one," she said and drew her blade before I even got off my scooter.

"Pushy," I said.

"You never know when trouble might show up at your door."

"What do you mean?"

She sighed and banished her blade. "We elders are blessed with many gifts. Some more than others. While I make no claims to having the ability of divination, I do often have a sense of a change in the winds."

"We're getting a storm?"

"Of sorts. The winds I spoke of are more of change." She walked closer to me and looked into my eyes. "Be careful in the times ahead. Change is coming for you. Times might get…difficult. Remember your training should you ever find the need for it."

I nodded and didn't like the sound of that at all. Change was never good. "I will, thank you."

"Come, draw your weapons."

And so we sparred for almost all of the two hours I had to spare. By the time we were finished, my arms felt like lead. I wasn't sweaty, and I wasn't dirty. I was just tired.

"Enough," she said and banished her blades. "I believe it is the custom of the humans in this world to 'take the weekend off' is it not?"

I laughed. "Yes. It is."

"Then I shall see you after two days' time. Enjoy yourself. Monday starts the difficult portion of your training."

"Advanced swordplay?" I had meant it as a joke.

"No, you are not ready yet. Maybe in a decade or so. Monday we begin training you on collecting souls."

I shuddered at the thought. "Great."

"More of your sarcasm, I see. Does not the thought appeal to you?"

"Not even a little bit."

"Good," she said and turned to leave.

I watched her walk to the edge of the woods. I had no idea where she went after she left me standing in the field every afternoon, nor did I dare to follow. Raven didn't seem to be the type to tolerate anyone spying on her.

I did have to admit, she was pretty amazing. I thought Darius was scary, but Raven made him seem…small. I guess being an archangel made you seem that way.

I smiled. I couldn't even imagine being that scary or having that much power. Although, being able to fling fireballs would be pretty nifty. I drew back my hand and threw an imaginary fireball at a large rock twenty feet away. I yelled,

"Whoosh," as I pushed with just a bit of power and imagined a fiery sphere hurtling toward it.

When the fireball impacted, it exploded and knocked me on my ass. The grass around it was scorched black and smoldering in the afternoon sun.

"Holy shit!" I scrambled to my feet and ran over to stomp out the flames.

I grinned after they were out. It was pretty cool, I had to admit to myself. But then the realization of what it might mean hit me. I glanced around to make sure I was alone before I bent down and let loose with a bit more magic, healing the grass and cleaning the rock that had taken the brunt of my experiment. The Fallen were already treating me a bit differently than before. I wasn't sure I wanted to add to their curiosity toward my abilities.

"The gods of parking are my friends tonight," I said to myself as I pulled into a parking spot right in front of the theater. It was Friday night, the mall was packed, the theater was packed, and I *still* got a primo spot.

I killed the tiny engine, grabbed the key, and walked up to the entrance, looking around for Jessie the whole time. It didn't look like she had shown up yet.

A line was forming at the box office and I was getting a little anxious. I would have gotten in line and gotten tickets for us, but I had no idea what she wanted to see. Glancing at the movie posters next to the box office, I groaned inwardly. There wasn't much I wanted to see. One shoot-em-up movie that didn't look to shabby, but other than that it was a collection of chick flicks, dramas, and one zombie movie.

I truly hoped that Jess didn't pick that one trying to make me more comfortable. I had *never* been a fan of zombies, zombie books, zombie movies, or even preparations for a zombie apocalypse. I didn't get everyone's growing fascination with the whole idea of people getting bitten by mindless undead creatures and then turning into ones themselves. To date, I had only ever found one book I even remotely liked. It was around Halloween and I had to do a book report on a zombie book. Jeremy had recommended some book called *Zombies Don't Cry* by some guy named Rusty Fischer. I had been *very* surprised to find I actually loved it. But then again, his zombies weren't mindless monsters. They were actually kind of cool, even if they ate brains.

A big black SUV pulled up to the curb and Jess hopped out before it even stopped moving. I heard her dad yell something at her and she briefly glanced in the door and yelled something back before slamming it shut.

Ruh roh. "Everything okay?"

"It is now," she said and gave me a hug and a quick kiss when she got close enough.

"What happened?"

"I don't want to talk about it. He's just being a pain in the ass."

I nodded in understanding. "What do you want to see? Your choice, it *is* the first movie you've seen in…"

"Longer than I can remember. I don't care what we watch as long as we have popcorn… How about… Um," she said as she quickly glanced at the selections.

Please don't say zombies. Please don't say zombies.

"Oh! Zombies it is!"

Crap. "Sounds good," I said with an inward groan. I grabbed her hand and we walked over to get in line. I snuck in a few more kisses while we waited. "What do you have planned for the rest of the weekend?"

"Absolutely nothing. Why?" I could hear the teasing in her voice. "Did you want to do something with lil' ole me?"

"Nope. Just wanted to see if you had something to occupy yourself with while I picked up a new hobby."

"You had better be joking. It could be hazardous to your health if you're not."

I smiled. "You caught me. What do you want to do?"

We moved up and were next in line to get tickets. The movie started in five minutes, and I honestly didn't care if we were late, but that would mean missing the previews, which might actually be better than the movie.

"Want to go Christmas shopping?"

"Um. Sure?"

"We only have a month. I need to start, even though I'm only buying for you and my dad."

"I've got you, the bratty sister, and my folks."

"Nothing for Claire?"

It's a trap! I could feel the tension building in the air as I formed a response in my head. "No. My friendship is gift enough," I said dramatically.

"You're such a dork. *My* dork. Don't forget it."

"Sheesh. Like you'd let me," I said with a wink.

The people ahead of us got their tickets and headed toward the theater door. We moved up to the window. "Two for *Zombie Paradise*, please," Jessie said and pulled out a credit card.

"I got it, Jess."

"No. Daddy does. His treat he said."

I nodded appreciatively. "Tell him I said thank you."

"I will, when I start speaking to him again." She signed for the tickets, grabbed them and my hand, and we went inside.

"Okay. Spill it. You're mad at him, fighting with him, and yet he still pays for us to go out," I said as we got in line for snacks.

"I said I don't want to talk about it–"

I silenced her with a kiss. "Okay. But at least tell me if it's bad. Should I be worried?"

"Oh. No. Not at all. He's just annoying me."

I laughed. "Well, remind me never to do that."

"Stay away from Shannon and all will be right with the world."

"I don't think you have to worry about that," I said and looked over at her with a smile, noticing the topic of our conversation standing at the entrance to theater three, the shoot-em-up movie I *wanted* to see. *Thank you for picking zombies. Thank you for picking zombies.* Shannon gave me a wink. I quickly looked back at Jess, hoping she wouldn't turn to see Shannon standing there. She started turning.

I panicked. "Will you marry me?"

"What?" She stopped turning, which was good, and smiled at me, which was not so good. It meant she was thinking about it.

"I suppose I should have said *would. Would* you marry me if we were older, not living with our parents, had good jobs, and a means to support ourselves?"

"Maybe," she said and ordered our popcorn, drinks, boxes of snowcaps, gummy bears, and cookie dough bits.

"Hungry?"

"Shut up," she said, giggling as she paid for everything.

Mr. James was rich compared to most people in Cedar Hills. I just hoped our trip to the movies didn't force him to mortgage his house. "Your dad is gonna kill us."

"I consider it penance for annoying me. Do you want a new car?"

"Jeez, when did you get so...*evil*?"

"Do you like it?"

I gave her my best "mad scientist" laugh. "Absolutely! It means my plan worked and I have corrupted the innocent!"

"You're such a dork."

"Yup. Yours. We already covered that."

"I'm going to pee quick," she said and left me to carry the pile of food she bought. I stuffed the boxes of candy in my hoodie pocket, tucked one drink in my arm, and grabbed the other drink and the tub of popcorn in my hands. I saw her duck into the women's restroom on the way to our theater.

I wandered over and hung out by the entrance, waiting for her. As I stood there, Shannon came out of the theater. The sounds of the movie playing blasted out the door as it closed behind her, only to be muffled again.

"Hi, Connor," she said and blew me a kiss as she headed toward the women's room.

"Hi…" I sighed and waited for the fireworks.

Jess opened the door, took one look at Shannon, glanced over at me, and slammed the door behind her instead of holding it open for Shannon.

"Wow. Bitch much?"

Here it comes…

But Jess ignored it. Or so I thought.

"Oh, Shannon," she said without turning around as she kept walking toward me.

"What?" Shannon turned, holding the now open door.

"You haven't even begun to see my bitchy side," she replied as she grabbed my face with both her hands and locked her lips to mine. I was grateful for the heaviness of the candy in my hoodie. It pulled it down well past my hips as I felt Jessie's tongue slip into my mouth. She didn't stop kissing me until she heard the bathroom door slam shut. "Ready?"

I nodded dumbly as I glanced down to make sure I hadn't dropped any soda or popcorn. "Yeah."

As hot as the kiss was…and as good as it felt… I felt a little used. I started to frown at Jessie, but then my little brain took over the thought processes from my big brain, and I gave Jessie a lopsided grin.

Jessie walked to the entrance to our theater, opened the door, and held it for me. "Sorry," she whispered as I passed.

"Don't be. I enjoyed that thoroughly."

"I figured you would. Is that a box of snowcaps in your pocket, or are you happy to see me?"

"Both actually."

Jessie laughed as she let the door close behind us, plunging us into darkness.

Chapter 11

My cell phone rang, waking me up from a very pleasant dream I was in the middle of. I reached over to my nightstand and grabbed it, unplugging the charger as I glanced at the screen.

It was two in the morning and it was my sister calling me. *What the hell?*

"Hello?"

"Connor! Come to the park, now!"

My sister's voice sounded panicked. "What's wrong? Are you okay?"

"No. Get here now. I need you," she said and hung up.

I jumped off the bed and slipped my cell into the pocket of the jeans I had fallen asleep in. I slipped my feet into my converse and grabbed a T-shirt on my way out of my room. I didn't even take the time to sneak down the stairs. Caelyn was in trouble. Getting to her was the only thought in my head.

Instead of taking my scooter, I leapt into the air and called my wings. The park was only a few streets over, and I could fly faster than I could drive.

The playground and surrounding fields were completely dark. That was unusual. The city usually left it well illuminated at night so passing patrol cars could keep an eye out for kids doing things they shouldn't be doing. A sense of dread filled me as I plummeted from the sky right near the swings. "Cae!"

I heard a muffled, "Over here," from the edge of the woods surrounding the playground. I headed that way, building speed with every step. I saw Cae first. She was crouched down on the ground holding something in her lap. When I got closer, I noticed it was Jenny. Elizabeth stood over them both in disbelief.

"What happened?" I crouched down to get a closer look.

Jenny seemed unhurt, but unmoving. "We were attacked," Caelyn said, muffling a sob.

"Is she okay?" I reached down and touched Jenny's wrist to search for a pulse.

"She's gone," Elizabeth spoke. She said it in a matter-of-fact tone that sent shivers down my spine.

"Tell me *exactly* what happened," I told Caelyn, not wanting to hear the deadness of Elizabeth's voice again.

"We were hanging out by the swings when the lights went out. We figured it wasn't a big deal and that they were on a timer or something. We could still see, so it didn't matter. All of a sudden, something landed behind us. I stood up, thinking it was you trying to scare us. I even yelled your name and told you to knock it off." Caelyn started sobbing and lowered her head until hers touched Jenny's.

"What happened, Cae? What happened to Jenny?"

Elizabeth spoke, continuing where my sister left off. "It had wings like you, but it wasn't you. I couldn't see it, even with my vampire sight. It was wrapped in darkness. I only know it had wings, because they stretched upward above it."

I nodded in understanding, waiting for her to continue.

"It went right for your sister. It grabbed her in both its hands and tried to fly away. Caelyn started screaming and kicking at it, but Jenny leapt onto its back, keeping it on the ground. The thing was strong. Stronger than us. It reached over its head and grabbed Jenny by the hair and flung her over its head. She landed about ten feet away."

Caelyn looked up and stared at me. "It was one of you."

"What happened after that?"

"I attacked it," Elizabeth continued. "Your sister broke free and ran for Jenny. She picked her up and took off for the woods, screaming at me to come on. I tried as hard as I could to get away, but the thing was just too damn fast," she said and started crying. It was one of those cries that you know won't stop until there were no more tears left. She couldn't breathe between the choking sobs. I walked over to her and took her into my arms, holding her tight. Caelyn kept talking.

"The thing started to do something to Elizabeth. I knew I had to help her, so I put Jenny down and ran back. I hit the thing as hard as I could, but it didn't even seem to faze it. That's when it touched Elizabeth's face with its hand. Connor, I saw it pulling her spirit…soul…whatever, right out her body. I did the only thing I could think of. I bit it. I bit it, started gnawing, and sucking its blood as fast as I could."

"What happened?"

"It let Elizabeth go. I grabbed her and ran the opposite way from Jenny, hoping it would chase us."

"Did it?"

"No. When I realized, we turned around and ran back. It was standing over Jenny and let a little blue sphere go before vanishing in the woods…"

I nodded, knowing exactly what had happened. I knew because I had done the exact same thing to Brett. "She is gone then."

Caelyn nodded. "I know. I can always *feel* when Jenny and Elizabeth are around. I think it's got something to do with me being able to feed on them. When we came back and I knelt down… I knew she was gone."

I kept one arm around Elizabeth and reached into my pocket, pulling out my cell. I dialed Clarisse. She answered on the fourth ring. "Clarisse, come to the park. We have a problem."

She hung up without answering and after a short while, landed not far from where I had. I called softly to her, knowing she would be able to hear me. She jogged to where we stood, looked down at Jenny and then back at me. "What happened?"

"She was attacked, by a Fallen. Her soul was taken."

"What did she do?"

Elizabeth straightened in my arms, and whirled on Clarisse. I could feel the anger radiating off her. "Nothing!"

"Why would they send a Reaper after her if she hadn't broken any laws?"

"It wasn't after her. It was after me," Caelyn whispered, fear in her voice.

"You don't know that," I said, but she shook her head.

"I do. It marched right through Elizabeth and Jenny to get to me. Why? What did I do?"

"I can't see why, you're not bound by the laws. Elizabeth and Jenny were. They promised their souls to become vampires and were bound by them. I don't get it either," Clarisse said, just as confused as everyone.

"What do we do now?" I nodded toward Jenny's body so only Clarisse could see.

"We need to call Darius. He needs to know what happened. The Reapers are his. He will also deal with…other arrangements."

I nodded. "How do we call him?"

"It's like opening a portal, but instead of… Nevermind. I'll do it," she said and walked back to the middle of the park. She looked up to the sky and I *felt* her call Darius. Quickly the sky turned to green and clouds began to swirl, forming a vortex above us. Darius fell from the blackness beyond and landed next to Clarisse. They spoke for a few minutes and he turned, looking in our direction. He paused momentarily before walking over to us.

"None of you saw who was responsible? None saw a face?" He sounded more worried than remorseful.

"No," Caelyn said.

He sighed. "I am sorry for your loss. We will find who did this. Connor, take your sister and her friend home. Clarisse and I will finish here."

"Finish?" Elizabeth stopped sobbing and looked at him in disbelief. "You mean clean up your mess. Our friend is dead and all your worried about is cleaning up?"

"Watch your tone, youngling. I regret deeply what has happened here. A promise was made to your friend that was broken by someone. We will find out whom. Until then, we must move on."

"Who? I'll tell you who it was. It was one of *you*. It had wings. That is what we saw."

I silently willed Elizabeth to calm down. The last person she wanted to enrage was Darius.

"We are not the only winged ones capable of doing something like this. Be careful not to place blame where it does not belong."

That bit of information surprised me. I had never even considered the Chosen having the same abilities as the Fallen, but it made sense. They were the same once, after all. "You think it was–"

He held his hand up for silence. His eyes said *not now.* I nodded in response. "Come on, Cae. Let's get Elizabeth home."

"I told mom I was staying over at her house tonight. I don't think she should be alone."

"Please," Elizabeth added.

"Okay."

I met Darius and Clarisse back at the park. They stood over where Jenny's body used to be. It was gone. "Where is she?"

"Her mortal coil has left this world, just as her soul has. She is no more. I will ensure that her parents' memories are altered."

"What does that mean?"

"It means her parents will wake up and have to face another day, knowing that their daughter ran away and they will most likely never see her again," Clarisse clarified.

"Wouldn't a little closure be better?"

"Finding their dead daughter's body would help?"

"I see your point. At least they can hope she is still alive."

"Fear not, Connor," Darius spoke again. "We will find her soul and it will have a place of honor among us. We owe her a debt."

"You can do that?"

"Her soul was promised to us. It should have found its way to one of our realms as it was released. Do not worry, we will find her. On that, you have my word."

"Do you think she'll know who did it?"

"You have never visited with the souls who come to our realm, have you?"

"No. The other day was the first time I had been there."

"You need to come home more. Find me when you return. You will have a place there for you should you need to leave this realm for a while."

"What do you mean?"

"He means you'll have your own apartment-like thingy. All of the Fallen have quarters in one of the realms," Clarisse interpreted for me.

"You have your own place?" I turned to her.

"Correction, I have two of my own places. One in Shade City and another one here."

"Most of the time I forget that you don't have parents and live by yourself. Doesn't that get lonely?"

"Sometimes," she said. I could tell by her face it was more often than sometimes. I fought the urge to give her a hug. It probably would have ended with her fist in my face, anyway. I turned to Darius instead.

"So, what were you saying about the souls?"

"That they usually have little to no recollection of their previous life. They also *never* remember their death. Often it is too painful a memory to bear."

"That makes sense. It would be on my top ten list of things to forget, anyway."

He nodded. "It is time for me to depart. If you have need, call me." He strode back to the center of the park and flew upwards once again, disappearing into the green vortex that appeared in the night sky.

"I can't believe nobody is going to call the cops about green swirling clouds above the park."

"Humans can't see it. Most of them anyway. The ones that can are usually already labeled by your society as different or insane. It's quite convenient."

"You and I have different ideas about convenience." The events of the night finally caught up to me and I swayed a little on my feet.

"Are you okay?" Clarisse reached out and steadied me on my feet.

"Yeah, Just tired. Want to sit with me a minute?"

"In the park?"

"Sure."

"We might want to get rid of our wings first. In case someone happens to drive by."

It was nearly four in the morning in Cedar Hills. Nobody would be driving by, but it is always better to be safe than sorry. I did as she suggested and followed her over to the swings that had already collected dew in the cool night air. I decided I didn't care about having a wet butt nearly as much as I cared about not falling on it.

I could feel it seeping into my jeans, chilling my backside even more that it already was. The cold no longer bothered me, but the wetness was a little uncomfortable.

"Feel better?" Clarisse wiped off her swing seat with her hand. She always was a little smarter than I was.

"Feels good to sit."

"Not what I meant, but I'm glad."

"What did you mean then?"

"About Jenny's soul. Death for humans is never permanent. For us on the other hand…"

"It is?"

"No one knows. When we die, we disappear. We hope it's to rejoin with the Creator, but that's just one of many theories by the Sages."

"Sages?"

"Yeah. I told you this before. We have many callings. Seekers and Reapers. You met Darius. Warriors, are the responsibility of Jun, whom you also met."

"And Agravius is in charge of the Sages?"

"Yes."

"What is a Sage though?"

"Wise one. They are our scholars."

"That makes sense. Who is in charge, charge of all the Fallen though?"

"No one person. It's the Triad. Three members so there is never a tie on any decision."

"And who do they report to?"

"I suppose the Creator, but he left these realms."

"He gave up on us?" I had a little trouble believing that.

"No! He is the Creator. He Creates. He doesn't oversee, or govern. He creates and lets his people thrive, or fail. But he loves us all the same."

"With that mentality, why the huge fight over free will? Couldn't it be considered the Creator's intention?"

"That is our argument, but the Chosen interject with the theory that the Creator made us to rule."

"Ahh. I see."

"Don't worry. You won't figure it out overnight. We've had millennia and we aren't any closer than we were in the beginning."

"Kind of like the Republicans and Democrats, huh?"

"Exactly. Except none of us are as evil as some politicians."

"One of us is," I said and nodded to where Jenny had been murdered.

"True. What bothers me about it is *no one* has broken the Truce since the Rift. To Reap a soul that didn't break the law is…" She let her voice trail off, letting me know that even she couldn't get a grasp of it.

"Well, it happened. Now we need to find out who did it and hope they don't do it again."

She nodded. "Keep a close eye on your sister. If she really was its target, it might try again."

"You're right. Can I ask you something?"

"Of course."

"Promise you won't freak out?"

"No."

"At least promise you won't hurt me?"

"Maybe."

It was as good as I was going to get. "How much do you know about Raven? The girls said the attacker was cloaked all in black. You've seen Raven. She makes goth look cheerful."

"She is one of the oldest of the old. She is, or was, one of the Dominions."

"What does that mean?"

"They were the middle hierarchy of the angels. Only the Seraphim, Cherubim, and Thrones had more power. They were the ones who were the administrators of the Creator's will. What was passed down, came to be."

"What do you mean?"

"Floods, famine, all the good stuff. Their power was, and still is, incredible."

"Then why is she teaching me, and why isn't she on the Triad?"

"The Rift. You know that the Usurper was a Seraphim, the most powerful of us all, right?"

I had heard that before and nodded. "Yeah."

"Well, after the Rift, most of the middle and upper hierarchy decided they were done with this plane of existence and left."

"You mean they committed suicide?"

"No. That is one of the greatest of laws. They just vanished. No one knows where they went. A few of them, such as Raven, stayed to advise, but they would never assume a leadership role. There is no trust among us that they wouldn't cause another Rift. That and they care little for anything anymore. They are not what they once were. So to answer your question if I think it could be Raven? My answer is no. She would have little interest in your sister, this world, or anything else. She probably only agreed to train you for a bit of a chuckle."

"Gee, thanks. The rest of it makes sense, though. Fighting takes it all out of you."

"Especially the Rift War. From what I hear, it was bad. Unimaginable bad."

"Gotcha. So when were you born?"

"A few millennia after. I was one of the last. Until you came along that is."

"And you were born a Fallen?"

"Yes."

"Where are your parents now?"

"You know Darius. My mother lives in another realm."

"Wait. Wait one stinking minute. Darius is your *father*?"

Clarisse chuckled softly. "He sired me. I don't know if you would call it being a father. We are not born helpless like human babies. We are not coddled. We are acknowledged. That is about it."

"That is kind of the saddest thing I've ever heard. Do you love your children?"

"Love." She seemed to think about it for a few minutes. "Not like you do. Down deep, we love everyone, but… We are more embracive to the more passionate emotions. Love, when you live forever, just like hate is an emotion better left unfelt."

"Okay. I take it back. *That* is the saddest thing I've ever heard. I kind of think I want to go home and hug my parents."

"I do, too," Clarisse said and laughed.

"Wait a minute! What about Mr. James and Jessie. He loves her with everything he's got."

"Once you throw a human into the mix, all bets are off. I'm sure he loved her mother, too."

"I know he did. Jessie told me all about them."

"It's different with humans."

"Why?"

"No one knows."

"Great."

"Alright, bedtime."

"Gee. Thanks, Mom. See. You're learning," I said with a wink. "Good night, Clarisse. Thanks."

"For what?"

"Answers and being here when I needed you."

She walked over to me and gave *me* a hug. I returned it, but when my arms slid around her, she pulled back. "Close enough, mister," she said and smiled.

Sean Hayden

Chapter 12

"Connor! Jessie's here!"

My sister's shrill voice echoed through the house and rattled through my teeth. "Okay!"

I pulled my shoes on and ran downstairs, seeing Jess and Caelyn chatting in the living room. From the amount of giggles I heard, I figured I was the topic of conversation.

"What did I do now?"

They both turned, looked at me, and giggled even harder. "Nothing," Jessie said, but I could tell she wasn't telling the truth.

"Uh huh. You ready to go, beautiful?"

"I'm not going," Caelyn responded innocently.

"You're also not beautiful," I immediately responded.

"Connor Sullivan. You take that back right now!"

I didn't know Mom was in the kitchen. She didn't sound too happy with my witty comeback. In fact, even Jessie didn't look too happy with it either."

"Relax everyone! Caelyn knows I'm just kidding. Right, Cae?"

She was looking down at her lap and sniffling. She said nothing. "Cae?"

"Connor!"

"Connor Ryan," my mom chimed in from the kitchen.

"Cae!"

She started laughing, and looked up at me and gave me an evil grin. "Yeah. I know."

I sighed in relief. "You're a brat. They almost killed me, you know," I said and pointed at Jess and Mom, who still didn't look too happy.

"Don't worry. I wouldn't have let them cut off much," she said and punched me in the arm before running upstairs.

"Sisters," I said to Jess, who only rolled her eyes.

"A good rule of thumb is to *never* tell a woman she's not beautiful. Even if she is your sister. Wars have started over that crap."

I nodded dutifully. "Consider it an oversight on my part, one that shall never be repeated again," I said and bowed low in a sweeping gesture.

"Smart boy. You ready to go?"

"Yep. You want to walk or take the scooter?"

"Oh, I have a surprise for you."

"What?"

"Come on. Follow me," she said and walked toward the front door. She opened it and pointed outside.

In the driveway was a shiny new convertible Mustang. "Holy crap. But wait. You don't have your license yet!"

"I do. Daddy took me after school on Wednesday. You were off doing something, so I decided to surprise you."

"Consider me surprised!" I pulled her into a hug and kissed her on the lips. "Did I mention I'm very proud of you?"

"Not yet, you haven't."

"Well, I am." I sighed heavily. I really needed to get off my butt and go get mine. Maybe then the parents would finally relent and let me get something bigger than a scooter.

The one problem with Jessie driving was that she was too nervous to let go of the steering wheel with both hands. Normally when we sat next to each other, her hand was in mine. Being this close and not doing it kind of bothered me.

"You okay?"

"Yeah. Just not used to not holding your hand."

"Don't worry, Mr. Clingy, we'll be at the mall in a minute."

"I know," I said defensively.

"Just so you know, I like that you're clingy," she said with a slight wink, taking her eyes off the road for just a moment.

That brightened my spirits enough to put a smile on my face for the remainder of the drive. It was only two minutes, as she said, but it felt a lot longer.

I growled when she got a spot right in front of the mall. "What is it with the women in my life and good parking spots?"

"You better mean your mother and your sister."

"Of course I do, Mrs. Clingy."

"Says the guy who can't even go five minutes without holding my hand."

"Good point."

True to her word, her hand was back in mine as we walked into the mall. It wasn't quite Thanksgiving yet, but most of the stores and even the mall itself were decorated with lights, holly, and bright colored ribbons. Even the Santa Encounter was being erected the last time I was there.

The sounds of Christmas carols wafted through the air. The smell of fresh pretzels assailed my nostrils, begging me to break my promise and pop their freshly baked, salted flesh into my mouth. I glanced over at Aunt Annie's and Shannon was nowhere in sight. I sighed in relief, but steeled my resolve not to even mention the word "pretzel" in Jessie's presence.

"They do *smell* good, don't they?" Jessie said timidly.

I played dumb. "What does?"

"Shut up. I know you can smell the pretzels."

"Oh, *those.* I guess. If you're into that sorta thing."

She swatted my arm and dragged me to the pretzel shop. I gawked at her like she was mad. "Relax," she said. "Shannon doesn't work here anymore."

Sean Hayden

"Huh?"

"She got fired."

"Huh?"

"Yeah. Someone called in an anonymous tip that she was giving free pretzels out to all her friends. Imagine that."

I stared at her as she ordered two pretzels and two cokes from the new girl behind the counter. "Wow," I finally managed to say.

"Didn't think I had it in me?"

"To tell you the truth, I'm just shocked that you didn't hire a hit man," I said and gave her a smile, truly impressed with her vindictive side that I hoped I never had to face in a million-and-a-half years.

"Daddy wouldn't pay for the hit man."

"Yeah. Might be hard to explain that on his American Express bill to his accountant."

We munched on our food as we wandered through the mall. Jessie left me standing outside Angelique's Closet while she went in to look at some items. Who they were for was a mystery. I kind of *hoped* they were for me. I just hoped she didn't expect me to wear them. I waved at Clarisse through the window and she nodded while she rang up an older lady. She shrugged, wondering what I wanted. I pointed at Jess who was looking at some revealing tank-top looking thingies. She smiled and went back to work.

I turned around and looked at a few of the shops around me, wondering if I could pick up anything on my shopping list. The trendy record shop that sold cult-series merchandise would be a good place to pick up some Dr. Who paraphernalia for my dad. I could even pick up some useless pretty thing for my mom at the Hallmark store. That just left Cae and Jess. I popped my head in to Angelique's and hissed at Jess. "I'll be next door."

I wanted to be quiet and not draw attention to the teenage boy sticking his head into a lingerie store. It didn't

114

work. Everyone turned around and smiled at my unwillingness to venture forth into the realm of lady's undergarments.

Jess nodded absently and I blushed my way out of the store, breathing normally as I finally made it out of sight. I made it all of twelve steps when I felt the *pull*.

I found myself turning in the opposite direction I had been going. Thoughts of Christmas presents were quickly replaced by a *need* to hurry to the other end of the mall. I couldn't explain it. I just had to be there.

Without running, I made my way through the hundreds of slow moving patrons doing their shopping. I heard someone briefly call my name, but I ignored it. I was on a mission, to do what I wasn't sure.

I finally slowed down by the food court. Nothing seemed unusual, just a bunch of people eating lunch or grabbing a snack. I scanned the crowd and found even more nothing. I shook my head to clear it, and turned to head back toward Jessie when it hit me again.

I spun and shot through the food court in a full run, bursting through the glass entryway and outside. Something was very, very wrong and I still didn't know what it was.

I quickly ran toward the sea of cars parked in rows, each person trying to park as close to the entrance as possible. The ground was littered with drink cups and food wrappers. I inadvertently kicked a few of them in my haste to get into the parking lot. My body kept being dragged farther and farther away until I was almost at the farthest row of cars.

I looked around. There were a few open spots, but not many. I kept walking the length of the last row until the *need* I had been feeling screamed into an alarm that rattled through me like someone had strapped a siren to my brain.

The feeling intensified as I drew closer to a ratty-looking green Ford that was probably older than I was. Whatever I was feeling was in there. My hand slowly reached out to open the door. I briefly wondered if the handle would

115

fall off if I touched it, but the door opened with a rusty creak. The windows had been tinted enough that I couldn't see inside, but with the door opened, sunlight poured into the driver's side of the car.

A young girl huddled in the passenger's seat and a literal monster loomed in the driver's. As soon as the door was fully opened, she screamed for help. The whatever-it-was turned toward me and snarled, drool dripping from its maw of razor-sharp teeth. It leapt onto me and I cracked my skull against the dirty asphalt beneath me. My arms shot up and I grabbed the thing by its shoulders, stopping it from biting my face off.

As soon as my hands touched it, I felt *everything*.

In my grasp was one Thomas Harding. He had wished to be a werewolf ten years ago. He lived in Johnsonville, which was nearly a three-hour ride from Cedar Hills. He hadn't come to our town to do any Christmas shopping, he had come to *hunt*.

For the past few years, he had been wondering what it would be like to feed off a human. He had started small, feeding off the wildlife in the forests that surrounded his town, but even the thrill of the kill was never enough. Deer blood was sweet, but he was sure human blood would be even sweeter.

The only thing that kept him at bay was fear. Only the fear of getting caught, not by the Fallen surprisingly enough, but by the police, stopped him from giving in to his whim. He held a disdain for the Fallen, finding them uncaring. Deep down he didn't think they would care if he ate a human or two, they probably just told him the laws to keep him from preying upon too many.

A missing person in a smallish town like Johnsonville wouldn't go unnoticed. He had watched enough television to know about DNA tests and such. With a limited amount of suspects, somehow or someway, he was sure to be caught.

Until he came up with the notion to hunt elsewhere.

The sleepy little town of Cedar Hills would be perfect. It was far enough from his territory he was sure he could get away with it. When he happened upon the mall and saw the young girl looking for her car in the farthest reaches of the parking lot, he knew he had found his next meal.

He watched her as she wandered around and then made his move when the lot was devoid of prying eyes. He grabbed her, put his hand over her mouth, and dragged her to his car. He forced her inside through his door and slipped in beside her, slamming the door behind him. He laughed at her as she tried to open the other door, which hadn't worked for years. Then he turned. Her screams melted into his ears like candy on his tongue. Her fear would make her flesh that much sweeter. He leaned in and licked her neck, from her shoulder to her ear. Sure enough, she did taste just like candy.

Suddenly, his door opened...

I blinked my eyes a few times to clear memories that weren't mine from my head. I stared at the snarling face in front of me in absolute horror and disgust.

This man was another Brett.

This man didn't deserve to have the gift that had been given to him. Then another thought crossed my mind that I prayed wasn't mine. *This man didn't deserve to live.*

My body took over.

My wings sprouted beneath me, lifting me from the pavement a few inches. My hands transformed, talons sprouting from my fingertips. They slowly sank into the flesh of the monster above me, totally preventing him from getting away. I felt a heat flow through my eyes. His expression told me everything I needed to know. My eyes were glowing red. He knew what I was.

He whimpered in fear as I released one of his shoulders and put my hand to his face. My magic poured down my arm and through my hand, pooling inside him and gathering his soul. His whimpers slowly faded from his throat as I pulled my hand away, dragging his soul out with it.

His soul looked like a blue, glowing translucent copy of his balding human self, not the monster he turned into. Its pitiful cries for help and mercy sounded like squeaks that would have been funny under any other circumstances.

I pushed his body away and kept his soul in my hand as I stood. When the last of it snapped from his body, the soul began to collect in upon itself, shrinking down in size and turning into a blue glowing orb.

"You broke the law, Thomas," I whispered to the globe and released it into the clear blue skies above me.

As it floated away, I turned back into my human-looking self and checked on the girl inside the car. She was staring at me like *I* was the monster, until it finally dawned on her that I had just saved her life.

"Thank you," she whispered as her eyes widened. I had a feeling she might be going into shock as the reality of what had just happened sank in a little more.

"You're fine," I said and caught her eye. I let my mind magic settle onto her gaze. "The man on the ground tried to abduct you, but he must have had a heart attack with all the excitement. Why don't you rest for a bit, and when you wake up, call the police and let them know what happened here."

"Okay," she said and lay back in the pleather seat, closing her eyes and dozing off.

I left the door open, looked around to make sure no one else needed to have their memories altered, and left to go find Jessie.

I slipped back into the mall and made my way back to Angelique's as fast as I could. I prayed silently that Jessie was still in there and not wandering around looking for me. I peered in through the window, hoping to see her there without any luck.

"Damn it."

"Damn what?"

I spun around. Jessie was standing behind me holding a shopping bag in one hand and her other on her hip, her stance slightly cocked.

"Er… Um…" I didn't even need to see the look in her eye to know she wasn't happy. Whenever a girl had one hand on her hip and was standing crooked, it was never good. I had been gone an awfully long time.

She started laughing. "What didja get me?" She glanced around my person, trying to see if I was holding any shopping bags. Her eyes narrowed. "Where were you?"

"Jess, do you honestly think I would walk up to where I thought you were shopping with a bag clearly labeled with the store's emblem where I bought your Christmas present? Do you give me such little credit?"

"Um… I guess so," she said with a smile. "Sorry. Just wanted to make sure you weren't getting me some video game or something for Christmas…"

"Would I do that to you?"

"If you thought I would grow an obsession over video games so I would be the *perfect* girlfriend, then yes."

"Sweetie, you're already perfect. If you played video games, my head would probably explode."

"Gasp! Are you telling me I don't already blow your mind?"

I could tell she was only playing. "Blow, boggle, scramble, frappe, and twenty other blender settings."

She laughed. "So where were you then?"

"Scouting."

"Like building fires and earning badges?"

"No. Scouting for the perfect gift for the girl who blenders my brain."

That earned me a kiss. "I love you, too."

"So… What's in the bag?" I tried to peer into it, but everything appeared to be wrapped in gold and white tissue paper.

"'Nunya."

"What's a nunya?"

"Nunya damn bidness," she said and gave me a light punch in the chest.

"I can live with that. Just answer me one question; are the items in the bag intended for me or are you buying them for other people?"

"Well, I guess you'll just have to wait 'til Christmas to find out."

It felt like the temperature of the mall rose several hundred degrees. "Okay then. Want to get something to eat?"

"Sure, but I'm buying."

"I can live with that, too."

Chapter 13

The school bell rang. Everyone rose at once and practically ran for the door. There was no sweeter sound on a Monday afternoon that the bell to go home. Under normal circumstances, anyway. While everyone else got to go home, play video games, and have a snack, I got to go to the clearing and have the snot beat out of me.

As I slowly walked to my locker, I thought again of Raven. While Clarisse and Darius were convinced of her innocence in Jenny's murder, I still had my doubts. While everyone might be considered innocent until proven guilty, the circumstances around the incident were just a little too convenient.

I opened the door to locker 636, stuffed what books I wouldn't need for homework inside, and slammed the door. I gave the dial a quick spin to make sure it locked and turned to look around for Jess.

She was walking toward me talking to Clarisse, which was a little strange. Clarisse was a senior and her locker was on the opposite end of the school.

"Hey, worm," she said as she and Jess got close enough to talk.

"Shouldn't you be somewhere torturing someone?"

"No. Torture Tuesdays. Today is Manicure Monday. I'm off to get my nails did before I have to get to work. See ya later. Bye, Jessie."

"Bye, Claire." Jessie slipped up next to me and slid her arms around me. "Want to come over?"

"I can't. At least not for a while."

"What have you been doing after school every day? You still haven't told me."

I panicked slightly. "Well. Your Christmas present isn't going to pay for itself. I've been doing some manual labor every day to save up."

Jess pulled back and stared up at me in shock. "Did you… Did you get a *job*?"

I laughed at her dramatics. "Yes."

"Where?"

"Doing some work for one of Dad's friends."

"Why didn't you tell me?"

"Hey, Jess. Guess what. I'm joining the workforce in order to purchase a Christmas present for you so I don't feel like a useless jerk of a boyfriend. See why I didn't tell you?"

She stilled for a moment and reached out with her hand, setting it on my arm. "Hey. You do know you don't have to buy me stuff right? I love you for you, not for Christmas presents."

Well shit. That made me feel like a total ass for lying to her. Telling her I had a job just seemed simpler than telling her I was being trained to reap souls and control my magic. "I know. I *want* to."

She nodded in understanding. "Okay. Don't work too hard. Call me when you get off," she said and gave me a quick kiss before heading out to her car.

I watched her go. I had been lying more and more to cover what was really going on with my life. It left an empty pit in the center of my stomach. *Just when I told myself I would always tell her the truth, too.*

I let the thought drift away. I was only doing what I had to do. I knew there was no way Jessie could know. Even if she turned into one of the Chosen, I don't think I could ever tell her exactly what I did as a Fallen. I didn't even like to think about it myself.

I stepped silently into the clearing, parking my scooter a good ways back into the thick woods surrounding it. I didn't see any sign of Raven, but then again, I rarely did.

I called my swords and walked inside, spinning slowly, waiting for an attack I was sure would come. I listened as well as looked. There were no sounds. No birds were chirping and even the wind, usually so prevalent in November, was still.

I felt her only seconds before she attacked from the one place I wasn't watching: above. She swooped down and landed, swinging her long sword down in an arc that would have cleaved my head like a pineapple if I hadn't crossed my swords above me at the last possible nanosecond.

"Good!" She stepped back and twirled, slicing at me from the side. "How did you know I would be attacking from above?"

I blocked her blade with one of mine and attacked with the other, which she easily swatted aside. "I *felt* you above me? Does that make sense?"

"Perfect," she said and attacked again with dizzying speed, her blade keeping pace with both of mine. "You're learning quickly."

"Clarisse was a good teacher."

"But I am better," she said and slammed one of my blades, twisting hers as she struck. Somehow, her move pulled the blade from my hand and it disappeared into nothingness as soon as it left my grip. She concentrated her attacks on my unarmed side. Reaching across my body to defend was difficult, but I managed. Barely.

I felt her blade slice across my arm, drawing blood. I hissed and brought my sword back across in a feeble attempt to strike her across her chest. My blade missed, but my second one, which I had called back into being mid-swing, didn't.

I felt the tip slow as it met cloth and then the flesh of her arm. Had it been the one holding her blade, she might have even dropped it. "Very good!"

Her wound didn't even slow her down.

If anything, it drove her forward in a frenzied attack that I had little chance of *seeing*, let alone defending against. "I can't!"

"You can. You're thinking like a human again," she said. "You're as fast as you think you are. Push yourself."

"I'd try if I wasn't so worried about being turned into hamburger meat!"

She stopped swinging her blade. I stepped back. "Fine," she said and banished her sword. She called two wooden sticks, vaguely shaped like my twin swords, into existence. She was ridiculously fast with one blade. She was a Cuisinart with two sticks.

She showed little mercy, either. I was battered by her batons multiple times before I even began to try to concentrate on what was happening. She pummeled my arms, sides, and even hands while I watched hopelessly. Her movements were a blur.

"Don't watch my blades. Watch my arms," she said and didn't relent with her attacks.

I did as she said. Instead of trying to follow the blades, I watched her forearms. I could tell the direction of her attacks and where to place my swords to block them. Her movements didn't slow, but they appeared to.

"That worked," I said as the sound of wood on steel echoed through the clearing.

"Good. Now I'm going to start to attack faster. Try to keep up."

She fell into a rhythm. Hack, hack, cross, and then a downward stroke. I didn't even think of moving to the offensive. I concentrated on following her movements. The sounds of our blades sped up and up, slowly though. She started sliding her feet to the right. We began to spin in the middle of the clearing, constantly facing each other as we weaved in an intricate dance. When both of us had become a blur, she changed the pattern of her attack. My eyes picked up her new movements immediately and my arms moved to match. She nodded her approval.

Then her attacks became chaotic, following no rhythm at all. She attacked with her left arm twice and then once with her right. I blocked all three. She switched the pattern and I parried every one. She became a whirlwind of movement and my body became a cyclone that matched her perfectly.

"You're getting it now. Instead of just blocking, add attacks of your own."

"I'll try."

Our dance picked up even more momentum. I tried to see openings where I could attack and saw none. At first. Slowly, I noticed gaping holes where her blades should have been and I realized she was using the obvious openings to help me see them better. The problem was they were gone before I could take advantage of them.

"You can see the openings, yes?"

"Yes."

"Then why didn't you attack me?"

"I'm not fast enough."

"Yes. You are. Don't ever forget that. Try again," she said and continued leaving gaps in her defense.

I brought my blade up to block hers. She opened her defense. Instead of moving my arm down to take advantage, I *willed* it. I imagined my hand moving at the speed of light and slipping my blade in the hole she had created.

It worked.

Her other blade left its place blocking my sword and moved to parry. "Perfect! I'll make a damn swordsman out of you, yet."

I felt the smile creep its way onto my face. She continued to leave openings, and I continued to take advantage of them until it became almost second nature.

"That's enough for today," she said and wound down her attacks until we faced each other, unmoving.

I was breathing heavy. Raven was not. I stared at her for a good long moment and just looked. She, too, was staring. I hadn't noticed before, but her eyes were red. Not glowing red, just red. It almost looked like she wore colored contacts. That tiny splash of red was the only bit of color on her.

"Can I ask you a question?"

"You just did."

"Another one."

She nodded. "Something is obviously on your mind." She tossed her wooden batons away and backed up a few paces. "What is troubling you, young one?"

"Did you reap a young vampire in the woods the other night?"

Her eyes widened in shock and then narrowed in suspicion. "I haven't reaped souls upon this earth in a *very* long time. Why would you ask?"

"My sister and two of her friends were attacked, even though none of them broke the Law. My sister's friend was killed. The Reaper wore all black."

"Ahh, I see. So you naturally thought it could be the stranger in your land, who happened to match the description."

"Just a thought," I said in my defense.

"And what makes you think I would admit to the crime?"

"You seem honest and you didn't know one of them was my sister. I thought you might…"

"Your instincts on my presumed response are accurate even if your instincts that I might have done the deed are not. Did you tell anyone of the incident?"

I nodded. "I called Clarisse and Darius. They told me it wasn't you and explained their reasoning. It seemed sound, but I can't think of anyone else who would even be a suspect."

"Leave it to Darius. He is the leader of the Reapers. He will find out who did it."

I nodded, sighed, and sat down in the cold grass, ignoring the sensation against my backside. "I will."

"Was she a friend of yours?"

I nodded. "She wasn't at first, but she became one."

"I'm sorry for your loss."

"Thank you. Are we going to practice magic?"

"Not today. You did quite well and I am very pleased. That is enough practice for the day. Tell me about your experience."

"What experience?"

"You reaped a soul this weekend, did you not?"

I nodded. "How did you know?"

She sniffed the air. "I can smell the soul. Part of its essence still clings to you."

I lifted my arms and sniffed my pits. I put deodorant on before I went to school. I could still smell that, but little else. "You can?"

"Yes. The twisted souls of those who break the Law leave a sour odor on everything they touch."

"I can't smell anything."

"Youngling, when you have lived as long as I have, you will. Don't forget, we grow in power as the centuries pass."

"We do?"

"Yes."

"That's kind of scary."

"It can be. Especially when those who do not wield their power properly continue to gain it."

"You mean me?"

"No. Another. Go home. Enjoy the rest of your day," she said and turned, crossing the clearing and vanishing once again into the woods.

I stood and made my way back to my scooter, mulling over everything I had learned and everything she had told me. The tiny doubt I had that she might have been the one who killed Jenny was long gone. I don't know why, but I believed her. Raven was scary, damn scary, but she also seemed sad above everything else. Sad and honest.

Sean Hayden

Chapter 14

The sensation of sunlight streaming through my window and shining on my face woke me out of my sound sleep. The smell of toast permeated my room and caused my stomach to growl intensely. I wasn't used to waking up on a weekday without an alarm blaring angrily at me for ten to fifteen minutes. I smiled. I loved holidays. Especially Thanksgiving.

I hopped out of bed, straightened my jeans, which had twisted around my waist while I slept, and headed downstairs. Cae was sitting on the couch watching the parade on TV. Mom was in the kitchen chopping onions and celery, and Dad was sitting at the kitchenette table with two toasters and six loaves of bread in front of him. I smiled. Dad always insisted on making the stuffing every year. I didn't have the heart to tell him, but it sucked. It was the consistency of wet concrete and gave me heartburn every year from the sheer amount of spices he encrusted it with. It did, however, *smell* awesome. Especially when it was cooking inside the turkey.

My stomach growled. *Turkey,* I thought and grinned, practically drooling down the front of my T-shirt. "Mornin'," I said, yawned, and made my way to the coffee pot.

"Since when do you drink coffee?" Mom was looking at me quizzically.

"I don't. But it smells good."

Her quizzical stare turned into one of utter bewilderment. "It's cold and three hours old. It's not coffee you're smelling. Your father probably burned some toast."

I shrugged, poured a cup, and popped it in the microwave for a minute. When it dinged, I pulled it out and sniffed the mug. "Nope, it was the coffee."

I set the mug down and looked at the black liquid. My experience with coffee was limited to caramel macchiatos and frappés. I had no idea how I liked, or even if I did like, regular coffee. Mom drank hers with cream and sugar. Dad drank his black. I shrugged and decided to try it Dad's way first. I could add non-dairy powdered creamer and sugar to it, but it would be a bitch taking it out if I didn't like it.

I brought the mug to my lips and ignored the burning sensation. I could take a fireball to the face and not get scorched. I doubted a little hot coffee would hurt me. I gulped some of it in my mouth and screeched like a little girl when it scalded my tongue. I rubbed it against the roof of my mouth until sensation returned.

"Careful, honey. It's probably hot."

I managed to refrain giving my mom a scathing look for winning the understatement of the year award. "Gee, thanks, Mom."

"Don't get pissy with me, mister. You're the dummy who decided to gulp scalding hot coffee."

I sighed. I hated it when she was right. "I know." I went to go sit next to Cae, snagging a piece of toast from Dad's table as I walked by.

"Hey. At least put some butter on it, you thief."

"Can't have butter, Dad." I was going to have to stencil it on their arms or something. With a tattoo gun.

"Is Jessie coming for dinner?" Mom had to yell over the sound of the announcers giving their float by float commentary on the television.

"No. She and her dad have a long time tradition of ordering Chinese food and watching movies. I told you that last week."

"Oh, yeah. Sorry. I forgot."

"It's okay."

"What about Claire?"

I could hear the apprehension in her voice. I don't think my mom was truly convinced that nothing was going on between her and I. "I didn't ask her."

"Connor Ryan, I raised you with better manners than that. You go call her this instant. Tell her to bring her folks, too."

My mother was one of those women who lived under the assumption that they had to make enough food to feed several small armies during the holidays. Unfortunately, every year when the holiday finally did come, she panicked about the amount of food she made and always extended last minute invitations to the surrounding neighborhoods, friends, friends of friends, enemies, school janitors, or anybody else she could find to help eat two twenty-pound turkeys. She never understood the concept of leftovers. "Okay, Mom," I said and pulled out my phone.

I sent her a simple text. *You're coming for dinner. Be here at 3*.

She replied with a simple, *K*.

"She's coming," I hollered over my shoulder.

133

Sean Hayden

"Mom made me invite Elizabeth, too," Cae whispered quietly.

"Isn't she eating with her parents?"

"They're eating at two. Her mom is the worst cook on the planet, so she jumped at the opportunity."

"How are the two of you doing?"

Cae looked over at me and I watched a single tear leak from her eye. She shook her head and I reached over and patted her arm. "I know," I said simply.

She nodded. "The parade this year sucks. It's the same floats from last year and they've had like twenty country performers."

I laughed. If there was one thing Cae hated more in this world than me, it was country music. I couldn't blame her. "Joy."

The day rolled by pretty quickly. The smells of turkey, stuffing, gravy, and the other twenty side dishes Mom made filled the house and made my stomach rumble. We didn't even eat lunch to keep our stomachs empty for dinner. At least we were eating early.

Clarisse showed up at exactly three. I was kind of shocked. She was never on time for anything. Except school. Sometimes. "Hey, worm, thanks for the invite," she said and strolled through the door carrying a bottle of wine. I followed her into the kitchen where she hugged Mom and handed her the bottle. "My parents told me to tell you that they were sorry they couldn't make it, but to give you that for taking care of me. Mom's working at the bowling alley and Dad is on duty this weekend. Hopefully nobody will burn their house down."

I laughed quietly. Clarisse had told my parents that *her* parents were a bartender and a fireman. It was actually kind of clever since the only things open on Thanksgiving were the bowling alley and apartment fires.

"Awww. What a shame they had to work," Mom said and hugged Clarisse again.

"It's okay. I'm used to it."

"Well, you're always welcome here, Claire," Mom continued. "And if you ever need a place to stay, we can put Connor on the couch."

"Wouldn't he be more comfortable on the porch?"

Mom started laughing, which only confirmed my suspicions that they were *both* evil. "Hardy har har," I said lamely and shot Clarisse the bird when Mom wasn't looking.

Dad saw me though, and cleared his throat. I gave him a sheepish grin. We left them to finish cooking the meal and went to sat on the couch. Cae saw Claire and got up to sit in the big recliner that was usually occupied for long stretches of time by my father. Why she thought I would want to sit by Clarisse, I had no idea.

"Hi, Claire."

"Whattup, squirt. How you doing?" She sounded light-hearted, but I saw the concern on her face as she got closer to my sister.

"Hangin' in there."

Clarisse gave her a smile and patted her head as she took the spot on the couch closest to my sister. That was good. They could chat about girl things while I watched the Somethingorother Dog Show. I didn't *want* to watch it; it was another Sullivan Family Tradition. It never ceased to amaze me how many stupid things we did on a daily basis in the name of tradition.

Sean Hayden

"What time are we eating? I'm starving and the house smells amazing."

"In an hour. We always eat at four."

"What have you been doing all day?"

"Pretty much sitting on the couch watching television. I went up to my room and played video games and contemplated the meaning of life for a while, but that got boring, too. What about you?"

"I organized my closets, took a shower, and did my nails."

"Sounds like you had even more fun than I did."

"Oh, yeah. Loads."

We were saved from having to converse further by the sound of the doorbell. "I'll get it," Cae said from her spot. "It's probably Liz."

"Anything else new?" I could tell by her whispered voice that she didn't mean anything in the mundane world.

"No. Just training with Raven."

"You asked her didn't you?"

"Yes."

"You're such an idiot. How did that work out for you?"

"Very well, actually. She explained that she didn't do it."

"And you believe *her* but not me?"

"She's a little more convincing than you are."

"True. She's scary."

"Very," I added and turned to see Liz and Cae greeting Mom and Dad.

"Since everybody is here, let's eat," Mom called to Clarisse and me.

I stood first and offered Clarisse my hand to help her up. She gave it a funny look before taking it and pulling herself to her feet.

"I'm not that old," she said.

"I know, but your walker is in the other room and I didn't want you to fall without your life alert necklace."

"That's so sweet!" She leaned in, wrapped me up in a hug, and promptly stomped on my foot.

I could actually hear the bones crunch inside my Airwalks. "*Ouch!*"

"Shut up. You deserved that one," she said and helped me into the kitchen.

"What's wrong, Connor?" Mom rushed over when she saw my limp.

"He accidentally bit his foot," Clarisse added helpfully.

"Oh, was it in his mouth again?"

"Up to the ankle."

"Well hobble over to the dinner table, sweetie," Mom said to me without an inch of compassion.

We sat as Mom and Cae started shuffling dishes full of steaming food and set it all over the table while Dad stood in front of his chair and carved the turkey with his usual ineptness. By the time he was done, it looked like someone had ripped the carcass apart with their hands while the bird was still alive. The only thing missing was the feathers and blood.

It did however, smell wonderful and I found myself drooling, waiting to get my hands on its succulent flesh. My stomach made weird noises that sounded vaguely like whale-song. I looked away from the turkey to see everyone had stopped what they were doing to stare at me.

I blushed. "Sorry. Hungry."

Mom rolled her eyes and the rest of them laughed. Dad tossed me a wing in sympathy. I started gnawing on it while the rest of dinner was brought out. Soon enough, everyone stood and joined hands. Clarisse looked at me quizzically. I mouthed the word *grace*.

She nodded in understanding and took my hand. Dad mumbled a few words about being thankful and bounties. I didn't really pay attention. I did, however, feel sort of uncomfortable during the ordeal. I made another checkmark in my mental "what's weird about being a demon" list. It was a good thing my parents weren't overly religious. I might have burst into flames or something. I looked over at Clarisse. She looked just as uncomfortable as I did. I think I even saw a bead of sweat on her otherwise perfect forehead.

Dishes were passed and plates were filled. We had just settled down to chow when the doorbell went off again. Mom looked up in surprise. "I wonder who that is," she said and stood to answer it.

"I'll get it Mom. You eat," I said and made my way to the front door.

I opened it. My girlfriend stood there looking very embarrassed. "Hi Connor. Is that offer for dinner still open?"

"Yes! Come in. What happened?"

"I called your phone but you didn't answer. Dad had something come up and had to cancel dinner and movies. You sure it's not too much trouble?"

I wrapped my arms around her and gave her a kiss. "Never. Come on," I said and took her hand and dragged her into the dining room.

Everybody seemed surprised and happy to see Jess. She had that effect on people. Everybody but Clarisse. I caught the look she was giving Jessie and it wasn't exactly what I would call "friendly."

Mom immediately got up and got her a plate. Dad dragged in a chair from the kitchenette set and made room between him and me. Jessie took off her coat and draped it over the back of the chair before sitting down.

"What do you want to drink, sweetie?" Mom opened the fridge and peered inside. "We have coke, milk, water, or juice."

"Water is fine, Mrs. Sullivan. Sorry for the lack of notice. Dad had something come up."

"Don't be silly. We're glad to have you. Now maybe Mr. Mopeypants can enjoy his dinner without sulking."

"I wasn't sulking! It was more of a pout," I added with a wink at Jess.

We ate and talked for what felt like hours. By the time we were done, I felt miserably full. I liked it. I felt the world fading as I slowly slipped into a turkey induced coma. I managed to mumble the word, "Couch," to Jess as I stood and waddled in that direction.

"I've never seen anyone eat so much in my life," I heard Mom say worriedly to my dad as I left the table.

"He's growing. Don't worry about it."

"Honey... He ate a *turkey.*"

"I used to eat four or five when I was his age."

"You're so full of shit."

I ignored their conversation and plopped down on the couch. I thought I heard it creak a little, but it was probably just my imagination. At least I hoped it was.

Jess sat down beside me and the rest of the girls filled up the room. "Movie?" Cae looked around the room to see if anyone was interested.

"Put it on," I said knowing Cae would catch my meaning.

There were exactly four Sullivan Thanksgiving Traditions. The parade, the dog show, stuffing ourselves silly, and finally, watching *The Nightmare Before Christmas.*

Cae grabbed the DVD and popped it in the player before sharing one of the large chairs with Liz. She hit the play button on the remote and the movie started. Jessie snuggled in closer and Clarisse plopped down on the other side of me.

"What movie is this?"

"The Nightmare Before Christmas," I whispered back to Clarisse. The beginning of the movie was my favorite part.

"I've never seen it."

"Me neither," Jessie chimed in, too.

"You're in for a treat. It's one of our traditions. To kick off the holiday season. Tomorrow we go buy a Christmas tree and decorate the house."

"Huh. I've never had one of those. We really don't do Christmas at my house. Dad is kind of funny that way."

I genuinely felt sorry for Jessie. I stroked her hair.

"Me neither," Clarisse said.

What was with the women in my life? I felt bad for Clarisse, too, but I refrained from stroking her hair. "Well, come over. Both of you. You can help and join in."

Both of them looked at me, smiled, and nodded. "Why don't they spend the night? I'll call their parents and let them know it's okay with your father and me, and that they will be spending the night in your sister's room. Under guard. In isolation. And that you'll be spending the night in the locked garage."

"Gee. Thanks, Mom."

"You're welcome, sweetie. Jess? Claire? Are you up for a Sullivan Family Christmas?"

"You bet. But you don't have to call my folks. They're both working and leave stuff like that up to me."

Mom nodded in understanding. "Want me to call your father, Jess?"

"He said he'd call when he was finished. I'll let you talk to him then."

"Okay. Mr. Sullivan and I will be upstairs watching TV. Come get me when he calls," she said. "Liz, you staying , too?"

Liz nodded and never took her eyes from the movie.

We watched in silence. Jess and Clarisse both were enraptured by the movie and I actually caught the two of them smiling, even during the musical numbers. If anyone asked me, I'd deny it, but I had *This is Halloween* on my iPod. It was one of my favorite songs and always reminded me of my favorite time of year.

The movie ended and we switched to some mind numbing TV shows. We looked for another movie to watch and failed miserably. Jessie's dad called after a while and Jess spoke a few words to him quietly before handing the phone to my mother.

"He said you could stay, sweetie," she told Jess before handing the phone back to her and looking over at me. "He also wanted me to remind Connor that he has several shotguns."

Dad started laughing from his seat in the kitchen where he and Mom were playing cards. "I'm going to have to get some, too."

"Don't worry, Dad. I was lucky to find Jessie," I said.

"I meant for your sister."

"I knew that."

"Connor, come help me get the sleeping bags and blankets out of storage. The girls can have a campout in the living room."

I nodded. "Good idea."

"And if I hear so much as a creak on the stairs, *I'll* borrow one of Mr. Sullivan's shotguns. Do we have an understanding?"

"Yes, ma'am."

"Good. I really wanted to see you graduate high school. It would be a shame to kill you now."

Chapter 15

The pounding on my door woke me up. I glanced over at my charging phone and saw seven am shining brightly. I groaned inwardly. *We were on a holiday, who the hell was pounding on my door before noon?*

"What," I wailed miserably at the door."

"Come on, honey. We're going to get the tree."

"The trees are still asleep, Mom. Go back to bed."

"We're doing something special this year. Come on."

"How about sleeping in? That was pretty special the last time I checked."

"Connor Ryan Sullivan. You get out of that bed this instant. Don't make me send your sister up here with ice and water again."

"She's still sleeping anyway. Or she would be if she was smart." I slid my head back under the covers. After the parents had gone to bed, we stayed up pretty late. I know Mom came out every thirteen minutes to make sure I wasn't being too huggy with Jess, so I knew she had to be half asleep, too.

"She is. I'm sending her up."

I listened to Mom's footfalls as she walked back downstairs. I strained to hear what was going on down there, but I couldn't make out her voice. I distinctly heard the words "ice" and "water" as well as the maniacal giggle of my sibling.

Sean Hayden

I cursed under my breath, got out of bed, walked over to the door, opened it, and shouted, "I'm up!" I slammed it and wandered around looking for somewhat cleanish clothes.

Two minutes later I was in the kitchen with one wide-eyed father, an over-planning mother, two vampires who were way more awake than they should have been, a confused looking demon, and Jess, who was as beautiful as ever and appearing quite amused.

"What the hell, Mom? What's going on?"

"We decided to do something special this year, since it will be more than the four of us. We'll drive up to Kildare and cut our own Christmas tree at the farm up there.

"When did you decide this?"

"When your father and I woke up this morning."

"Old people are weird," I mumbled and hugged Jess before grabbing the last of the coffee out of the pot. Learning my lesson from the day before, I sipped it slowly. It wasn't as hot as straight out of the microwave, so I gulped it down greedily before tossing the plastic mug that said, "World's Best Dad," in the sink. "I'm ready."

The seven of us piled into the parent's minivan and once again, I was sandwiched between Jess and Clarisse while Cae and Liz got the whole back backseat to themselves. It wasn't that I minded the proximity to Clarisse, but some alone-time with Jess would have been nice. I shot my sister a dirty look, wanting the backseat for just that purpose.

"Don't look at me, Mom said if you and Jess made for the back to kick out your kneecap. She wants you where she can watch your hormonal ass."

I sighed in frustration and turned back around. Mom shot me a smile from the front seat and Clarisse lost it, laughing loud enough to actually hurt my ears.

The drive took a little over three hours. My ass was numb and my palm was sweaty from holding Jessie's hand the entire trip. Dad finally announced, "We're here!" The rest of us began clapping.

There was no snow on the ground, but we were still in the spirit of the season. The early-morning air was calm, quiet, and chilly. It couldn't have been more perfect as we piled out of the minivan.

The owner of the tree farm walked out of a large wooden barn to greet us. "Mornin', folks. Looking for a tree?"

"Yes, do you have any here?" I tried not to sound sarcastic, I failed miserably. Luckily he had a sense of humor.

"First time I heard that joke. Good one," he said and winked at me.

I had the decency to blush. Clarisse still smacked me in the back of the head.

"Thank you," Mom said to her appreciatively.

"You're welcome. Let me know if you need me to take him out back and kick the crap out of him."

"Maybe later, sweetie."

I felt Jess' quiet giggle more than heard it. I looked down at her and she refused to make eye contact. "You, too?"

"What?" She tried sounding innocent.

"I heard you giggling over there."

"Love you," she said simply and smiled, finally meeting my eyes.

"Love you, too."

"You two are gonna make me barf my nonexistent breakfast," Cae felt the need to chime in.

I kissed my girlfriend soundly.

Dad's conversation with the tree farmer was interrupted by dry-heaving noises emanating from my sister. "Knock it off, both of you."

"She started it…"

The clouds had rolled in, darkening the bright morning light. A solitary break let the sun stream through in a cone of brilliant hues that sparkled in the lonely rows of trees. A shaft of light illuminated a solitary tree, somewhat separated from the others. It was as if the heavens themselves had picked the Sullivan Family Christmas tree.

"How about that one?" Dad sounded almost reverent as he spotted the beauty before us.

"Perfect," Mom echoed behind him.

Dad hefted the axe the farmer had loaned him, and strode forward, leaving the rest of us behind. He spit into his gloves, grabbed the handle, and whacked it good about eight inches from the base of the tree. The axe bounced off after making a small dent in the bark.

"We're gonna be here a while," I said with a little laugh.

Mom walked over to Dad. "Is it sharp enough?"

"Yeah. I checked it before we left. It's just a tough tree."

"Let's pick another one then."

"Hell no. It's this one."

She sighed, rolled her eyes, stepped back, and let him have at it. Thirty minutes later, he was only a quarter of the way through it.

"Why don't you give your dad a hand, Connor," Clarisse whispered next to me.

I nodded, the novelty of standing in the middle of a freezing forest having worn off long ago. "Take a break, Dad," I said and grabbed the axe in his hand.

"No way, kiddo. This sucker is tough. You'll chop your foot off or something."

I rolled my eyes and pulled on the handle anyway. "Just a small one. I'll be careful and you need a break. Go warm up."

He let go reluctantly. "Chop on an angle. Watch for bounce-backs, and keep an eye on your shins."

"Yes, Father," I said and waited for him to join the others. I gripped the axe in both hands, settling the blade in the groove he had made in the trunk. Slowly, I pulled back until the axe was behind me. I swung with everything I had.

"Connor!" I could hear the panic in Dad's voice as the axe swung in a perfect arc toward the trunk.

The axe head hit the trunk, exploding it into shards of wood and bark as it continued travelling through and embedding itself in the dirt to the left of the tree. The tree dropped back onto the stump and toppled over, nearly landing on me in the process.

Everyone behind me began clapping in anticipation of going home. I turned and saw my mom and dad standing there with a look of utter confusion and awe on their faces. I shrugged my shoulders and hefted the axe over my shoulder.

"Jesus, Connor."

147

"Lucky hit, Dad. You loosened it up for me. Thanks."
"No problem, son.

Chapter 16

We pulled into the parking lot of the family diner with the tree–that was way larger than it looked while standing upright in the forest–strapped firmly to the roof of the minivan. We drew a few looks from the people getting in and out of their cars, but it was worth it. I was still feeling pretty good about myself for felling it with one stroke of my axe. I sort of felt like Paul Bunyon. Without the ox.

We walked inside and the place smelled awesome. Greasy, but awesome. The smell of bacon permeated the restaurant like a heaven-scented air-freshener. "Mornin'. How many?"

I looked up at the ancient waitress in her pink uniform and smiled. She even had a nametag that read *Flo*. That earned a giggle. The place was my new favorite restaurant. "Seven," I replied for Dad, who was still trying to get inside the door.

"Follow me, hon."

"Thanks." I took Jess' hand and followed. She had to be in her late sixties, but she sashayed with the best of them. Jess smiled and buried her face in my arm.

She led us to a large round table in the corner. We sat and she handed us each a sticky laminated, single-sheet menu. "The Porksplosion is the special for today. Holler at me when you're ready to order."

She sauntered off, refilling coffees and taking more orders. I looked around. The place wasn't that small, yet she seemed to be the only waitress in the place. "Wow. She must be good."

"Huh?"

I looked over at Jess. I hadn't realized I had been thinking out loud. "She must be good. She's the only waitress in the place."

"Oh." She looked around, and shrugged, seemingly unimpressed.

I looked at the menu and my eyes found the Porksplosion, which was a combination of three eggs, toast, hash browns, bacon, ham, and sausage. "Nom noms."

"What is?"

"The Porksplosion. I'm starving."

Her eyes widened at the description. She looked over at me, down at my belly, and back up to my face. "You're gonna get fat. I'll still love you, but you're gonna get fat."

I touched my belly, which was harder and flatter than ever. There was one good side to being a demon, unlimited caloric intake. I could eat with the best of them and not worry about ending up on an eating intervention show.

"Everybody ready?" We all nodded at Dad and he waved Flo over to take our order. Everyone ordered smallish breakfasts, except for Dad, Clarisse, and me. We all went for the gold and ordered the Porksplosion. We all grinned at each other after Flo left. The rest of them rolled their eyes.

Caelyn even said, "Men!"

Clarisse laughed. "Lightweight."

"I don't want to look like a bloated tick."

"Not like you ever would…" She trailed off, remembering Mom and Dad sitting at the table. At least she didn't make any blood-sucker jokes.

I glanced over at Jess, who was staring down at the white Formica-covered tabletop, not really paying attention. I nudged her, gently. "You okay, baby?"

She seemed to snap out of it. "Yeah. Just feeling a little weird."

"You getting sick?"

"No. I don't think so."

"Good. I don't like it when you're not feeling good," I said and leaned in for a kiss. She pecked my lips and sat back in the chair.

The sound of glass breaking drew everyone's attention. Somebody knocked a glass onto the floor at the table next to ours. Everyone in the restaurant started clapping, drawing laughter from all of us. Except for Jess. She sat there with her hands covering her ears and grimacing in pain. I touched her arm gently.

She glanced up at me, tears rimming her eyes. Her eyes began darting around the restaurant. The moved from an elderly gentleman tapping his glass with his fork to a trucker who was repeatedly rapping is knuckles against the countertop in the front. I could see the panic on her face. I gently grabbed her arm and helped her to her feet, leading her out of the diner and into the relative quietness of the outdoors.

She calmed as she closed her eyes. The only sounds around us were a few birds in the trees and the distant sounds of cars cruising down the highway. "You okay?"

She nodded. "Must be a migraine coming on. It was too noisy in there." She closed the distance between us and rested her face against my chest. I wrapped her in my arms and kissed her head, slowly swaying in an effort to calm her.

"I think Mom has some aspirin in her purse. We'll get you some in a minute."

She nodded, not looking up. Clarisse came outside to check on us. "All good?"

"Yeah. She's getting a migraine and the noise of the diner was getting to her."

Clarisse opened her mouth to speak and quickly shut it, shooting me a worried glance. I scrunched my eyes at her in confusion, raising one eyebrow. She looked around before bringing her hands up to her shoulders and making flappy gestures.

"Oh," I mouthed silently.

She nodded at my comprehension, bringing two finger tips to her eyes and then using them to point to Jess. The universal sign for, "Watch her and make sure she's not turning into a Chosen."

I gulped silently. Jess looked up at me, and then turned around to see Clarisse re-enter the diner. "I see why you two are friends."

"Huh?"

"You're very much alike."

I smiled down at her, actually taking that as a compliment. "Told you she's not that bad once you get to know her."

"I didn't say I like her. I just said you were a lot alike."

"But…"

"It's got nothing to do with *her*, sweetie. She's a girl, she's disgustingly pretty, and she's not related to you. There's a jealousy issue. It can't be helped," she said and gave me a feeble apologetic smile. "Sorry."

"Don't tell anyone, but it's kind of hot when you get jealous," I replied with a wink, kissing her lips softly.

"You're strange."

"But you love me."

"Most of the time." She pulled back a little and smiled, letting me know she was teasing. "I'm better. Ready to go back in?"

"Hell yeah. I have a Porksplosion waiting for me.

"I'm telling you… Fat."

"That's one thing I can promise you will never happen."

"So he says now. I'm not buying you new belts though."

After shaving about three feet off the bottom of the tree, Dad finally got it into the stand without it hitting the ceiling. There still wasn't any room for the star, but he said he had a plan. Mom rolled her eyes and grabbed the girls to help her pull the decorations out of the basement.

"Everything okay with you and Jess?"

I looked up at my father in confusion. "Yeah. Why? Doesn't it seem okay?"

"Yes. I don't know why I asked that. Maybe just making small talk with my son?"

"Jeez, Dad. Pick a different subject next time. You're gonna give me a heart attack."

He had the decency to look apologetic before he started trimming stray branches and shaping the tree. I flipped on the television and switched to the Sounds of the Seasons on the music channels. There was something important about listening to Christmas music while decorating the tree. Without it, it was like decaffeinated coffee. Or turkey bacon.

"Here's the lights, hon," Mom said as she deposited a box on the floor next to Dad before turning around and heading back downstairs.

"Come on. Help me check these."

Thus began my hour of hell. I silently vowed to myself to buy new Christmas lights every year when I was older. It just wasn't worth it. If I weren't a Fallen, my fingers would have had blisters from pulling the little green thingies out of the green pluggy things. I was about three seconds away from snapping. Miraculously, the last strand Dad and I were working on flickered to life. I sighed and stood. The lights went out.

"I quit!" I left amid a chorus of giggles where the girls were sorting through the boxes of Christmas cheer. I felt like stomping on an ornament. "I'm taking a break. Want to go outside, Jess?"

She looked over at my mom, who nodded. "Go ahead, sweetie. Maybe you can put him in a better mood."

"Sure," Jess said and grabbed my hand. I pulled her to her feet and headed toward the back door through the kitchen.

The cold air helped my mood a bit. Jessie in my arms helped a lot more.

"So... How are you liking your first Sullivan Family Christmas?"

"You have no idea how perfect you have it, do you?" She looked up at me solemnly, a tear forming in the corner of her eye.

"Excuse me?"

"It's been just me and Dad for so long, I forgot how holidays were meant to be spent. Be very thankful."

"I am. But I'm more thankful that you're here to spend it with me, too."

"You're a suck."

"Is that a bad thing?"

"Never. Just don't stop."

I leaned in and gave her a quick kiss. "Ready to go decorate a tree?"

"Yep."

Sean Hayden

Chapter 17

The door to the school opened and I could smell Monday wash over me like a bad bean burrito fart. I groaned as I passed through the entrance and into the halls of monotony. Even the sight of Jessie, waiting for me by her locker, couldn't brighten my outlook of another week of school. I didn't think I could handle the two weeks we had left until winter break.

"Hey, handsome."

"Hi, beautiful. Happy Monday."

"It'll go quick. Just stay out of trouble," she said with a wink and a smile.

"Did you just meet Connor?" My sister's voice echoed from behind us. I turned in time to see her roll her eyes as she passed us on her way to class.

"Not my fault it finds me," I called after her.

"Come on. We're gonna be late," Jess said and pulled me by my hand toward homeroom.

All in all, the morning passed rather quickly with a minimal amount of suckage. If only the day had stayed that way.

Sure, I was looking forward to having lunch with my beautiful girlfriend, and lunch started normally enough with us getting into line, ordering our usual salad and lunch with meat-like products for me. It was hamburger day, which are slightly less dangerous than sloppy-joe days.

We had just sat down and started eating when the unthinkable happened. By unthinkable, I mean the worst possible thing in the universe that could have happened, happened. No, the sun didn't go supernova turning the earth into a fiery ball of destruction and killing all life on earth. My girlfriend did.

Shannon had exited the lunch line and deposited her tray and drink at her table a few rows away. Picking up her banana, she glanced at it, made a face, and decided it wasn't worthy of her consumption. She headed toward the garbage can which was inconveniently located on the opposite side of *our* lunch table.

Jess tensed as she approached. I gently reached over and placed my hand on her knee and as she turned to look at me, I gave her a little smile. At the same exact moment, Shannon walked past, running her fingertips over my shoulders seductively.

The color drained from my face as I watched Jess' anxiety turn to anger and then morph into fury. I think I whispered, "Oh shit," as Jess stood violently. I heard the crunching of plastic and looked down to see the bench she had been sitting on shatter as her knees drove it backwards when she stood.

I was going to have to take one for the team.

In an effort to avoid a full-scale massacre in the James Underwood High School cafeteria, I stood, wrapped Jess in my arms, and practically dragged her through the maze of tables and out the door into the courtyard outside.

"Don't you dare stop me!" Her voice echoed between the buildings and I'm sure was cutoff mid-sentence as the doors leading inside closed behind us.

I pushed Jess back to arm's length and looked into her beautiful green eyes. I could see nothing but hatred. Hopefully it wasn't focused at me. "Do you really think she's worth it? Think about it. If you hurt her, you're going to get into serious trouble. Do you know what your dad would do to you? Do you have any idea how long you'd be grounded for?"

"I don't care! And I don't understand why you're stopping me! What? Did you *like* it?"

Uh-oh. The conversation turned in a direction I hadn't even considered. "Are you crazy? I love *you*. Why the hell would I want her to touch me?"

"Did you just call me crazy?"

"No. I asked if you were. Big difference. But the way you're acting, I'm starting to…"

Yeah… Not my crowning academic achievement. I might have mentioned in the past that I wasn't the brightest bulb on the strand. I didn't even get to finish my sentence when her knee shot out and found a new home, nestled snuggly at the juncture of my legs, displacing my small family of two. My girlfriend had just kneed me in the nads. My world collapsed inwardly as did my intestines and other organs as the wave of pain swept upward.

Apparently, even the Fallen weren't immune to a well-placed nut-shot.

I dropped to my knees as my eyes closed and a song of anguish escaped my lips, filling the courtyard with its forlorn melody of despair.

"Asshole," she said and took off toward the cafeteria.

"Jess. Wait!" It took everything I had to get the words out. It didn't help. I watched her back as she threw the door open and walked inside, leaving a small trail of white feathers in her wake…

Things went from worse to abysmally horrid in the blink of an eye. I sucked it up and stood, a little wobbly I admit, but at least I was on two feet. I hurried after her, expecting a war of cataclysmic proportions on the other side of the ancient glass door.

What I got was Jessie standing in front of Shannon, visibly shaking and shouting the words, "If you want him, you can have him!" She stormed off and headed back toward the classrooms.

The students in the lunchroom, who had completely given up on eating to watch the drama unfold, visibly shrank as Jess walked by their tables.

I, on the other hand, could feel my heart breaking as I watched her walk away. I sank back to my knees, not caring that my jeans were touching the floor of the lunchroom, the floor that probably carried every bacteria known to man in one convenient linoleum covered petri dish. I forgot about the pain in my nuts as the pain in my heart became the new center of my universe.

I don't know how long I stayed there either. Eventually, I felt a pair of hands grip under my arms and lift me to my feet. Feminine arms embraced me as I felt someone's breath on the back of my neck. I started to spin furiously, fully expecting Shannon to have mistakenly claimed her prize, when Clarisse's voice whispered softly into my ear.

"If you don't want to make the biggest mistake of your life…go after her."

And with those subtle words of wisdom, she let me go.

My sneakers squeaked through the hallway sounding like a basketball game as I raced after my girlfriend. At least I hoped she was my girlfriend. I had never seen her that angry. I hoped to the Creator that I never saw her that angry again. Ever.

I saw a flash of red head up the stairwell to the second floor. Since Jess was the only girl in the school with that exact shade of hair, I gave a full fledge burst of Fallen speed and made it to the stairs within moments. Footfalls echoed on the flight above me. For a nanosecond, I debated calling my wings and jumping. Then common sense took over. Landing next to Jess with glowing eyes and leathery wings probably wouldn't be a good idea.

I did use my speed to take the stairs three at a time, and I caught up to her at the top. "Jess! Wait! Please…"

She stopped running, but didn't turn around, continuing on her way toward American Government without looking back at me.

I reached out my hand and put it on her shoulder as I fell into step behind her. "Please," I whispered again.

She stopped. She still didn't turn around, but stopping was a good sign. "What?"

I could hear the anger edging her voice like a sharp knife. I knew it was sharp, because it had already cut my heart. "I owe you a very large apology."

That got her to turn around. My heart went from cut to shattered with one glance at her face. Tears streaked her face, smudging her makeup, highlighting the sadness in the depths of her eyes. She collapsed against me, burying her face in my chest and sobbing uncontrollably. Wrapping her in my arms, I did the only thing I could do, I held her tight.

"No… You don't. I'm the one who's sorry," she managed to blurt out between sobs.

"For what? I should have just let you kick her ass. God knows she deserves it."

"Why?"

"Why what?"

"Why does she have to want you? We were so happy. Why *you*?"

"Well, I am awfully sexeh…" I let it hang out there to let her know I was joking.

"Not funny," she said and rubbed her face against me some more.

"Gasp! You don't think I'm sexy?"

"Connor, you are like the hottest guy in the school. When I first saw you, my jaw dropped open. I can't believe you were single when I met you. I mean, why does she have to make a play for you *now*?"

I pulled Jess away from my chest and tilted her head up so I could look into her eyes. "It's probably my fault. You have no idea how much shit I took from her in the past. I think she knew I should hate her for it, but I felt sorry for her. When she was having a bad moment, instead of taking advantage of it and making her feel worse, I was actually nice to her. I should have kicked her when she was down. I think she misinterpreted that as interest."

"Are you?"

"Am I what?"

"Interested?"

"In spending the rest of my life with you? Yes. In ever spending another moment of time in her presence? I think I'd rather be dragged by a taxi over a mile of thumbtacks."

That earned me both an *awww* and a giggle. I kissed her lips gently, ready for her to pull back if it was too soon. It wasn't. She wrapped her arms around my head and mashed her lips against mine. "I don't know what's wrong. I haven't been myself lately."

My mind flashed to the trail of feathers she left in her wake when she ran from me in the courtyard. I needed to talk to her dad. I didn't have one doubt in my mind that she would be sprouting wings at any time.

I gave her my best reassuring smile. "No jokes. Please… Please believe me when I tell you I have zero interest in anybody but you. You are my reason for waking up in the morning. You are my reason for coming to school every day. I would never do anything to betray you, hurt you, or even make you sad."

The tears started flowing freely again, but this time, they were accompanied with the cutest little lip quiver and the brightest smile I had ever seen.

"I love you, Connor Sullivan."

"I love you, too. Future Mrs. Sullivan," I said with a wink.

Her eyes went a little wide. "Um…"

"Jeez, Jess. I'm not talking next week. You know. In a decade or so. When we're old and grey."

"Okay," she said with a relieved smile.

"Sweet. I'll post the engagement in the paper next week. Maybe that will give Shannon the hint."

163

"If that doesn't work, there's always the crowbar in my dad's trunk…"

I reached out and tilted her chin back up to me. "She is sooo not worth the effort, sweetie. You stay away from her and hopefully she'll stay the hell away from both of us."

"Fine. I will."

I didn't like the sound of that. "What?"

"Nothing," she said with an impish smile. I rolled my eyes and gave her another hug, just as the bell behind us rang. The sound caused Jess to jump in my arms, bringing her knee in contact with my lower extremities, yet once again. It caused me to hiss and wince in pain. I took an involuntary step backward and bent over, just a little.

Jess gave me one look and knew exactly what was troubling me. "Oh, my God. I am sooo sorry! How the hell were you running after me after what I did to you?"

"Cuz the thought of losing you hurt worse. Now it's catching up to me…"

"Let me go get you some ice!"

She turned to run and I reached out and grabbed her hand. "It's okay. I'll be fine in a minute."

The fact of the matter was, I should have *already* healed. I thought I had until the slight brush of Jess' knee brought a wave of pain rushing back. I guess it didn't matter if you were immortal or not, the boys were just gentle no matter what species you were.

Chapter 18

Raven attacked before I even swung my leg over my scooter. Albeit, I was moving a little slowly from my earlier groin injury, but didn't the rules of battle etiquette demand waiting until your opponent was ready or something chivalrous like that?

I only had one option. I rolled off the side of my scooter and kicked her away from me while pulling my blades from nothing.

"Good! Although, I will admit, I could have struck you down just then."

"Yeah. I had my mind on something else and I wasn't expecting you to attack me while I still had the motor running."

"A sword waits for no one!" She charged and swung low. I used one blade to defend and took the initiative to attack with my other hand. This time I didn't swing, I pictured my hand moving instantly from where it was to her shoulder. When the blade sliced into her flesh, I gave a gasp and dispelled my blades.

"Holy shit, Raven! Are you okay?"

"It will mend in a moment. Call back your blades!"

She actually seemed excited. I knew the Fallen were pretty weird, but this took the cake. If someone had sunk a blade halfway into my arm, I'd be crying like a little girl. But I did as she asked and called my blades back just in time.

Raven didn't hold back, nor did her injury seem to impede her ability in any way, shape, or form. My eyes could barely see her movements and I concentrated on her forearms like I had before.

She was graceful, amazing, and scary. Everything I wasn't. I felt choppy and inadequate every time we faced off. I took a deep breath while I blocked three of her well-placed attacks and pictured my movements flowing like water instead of just moving parts of my body. Instead of hacking, I started swishing. It worked.

Raven increased her speed.

I flowed to match.

"Incredible!" The smile that had found its way onto her stony face was almost…attractive.

"What?"

"Do you realize you are moving double of what you were last week?"

My eyes went a little wide. To be honest, I couldn't tell, nor could I possibly understand how *she* knew. "Are you sure?"

"Youngling, I have fought aged warriors who couldn't move this fast. I admit, I am most impressed with you!"

"Probably not as much as I am."

She gave a short bark of laughter. "I would say our time together from this moment would be short, but I am rather enjoying myself."

"It is kind of fun."

"Then I shall teach you to dance!"

"Exqueez me? I don't…dance."

"And a short time ago, you didn't swordfight either. Follow, youngling." And with that she crossed her one foot over the other and turned, forcing me to do the opposite or leave my side open to attack.

The whole time she moved, her blades never stopped their blurring parries and slashes. Two turns to the left and one to the right and we would begin again. I could almost hear the symphony in my head as we weaved and bobbed in a deadly dance. The whole time, the smile never left Raven's face.

Finally it drew to a close and her attacks slowed until her hands came to rest at her sides. She beamed at me in appreciation.

"Thank you."

"For?"

"That. It has been a long time since the teaching of others has brought me even a modicum of joy. In fact, when I was asked, I almost turned down the role. Something nagged at my conscious this time and so I agreed. I am not disappointed."

I blushed furiously. "Thank you, Raven."

"That is enough for today. Do you still wish for me to be your mentor? I admit, I have little else to teach you in the way of the blade."

"Yes. Definitely."

"Good. Practice does make for perfection."

"Actually, there is more to it than that." I had to tell her about being able to throw fire. It was a power that I shouldn't have, but that seemed to be the norm lately. I don't know what drove me. I had secrets I didn't want learned, yet I trusted her implicitly. She just had that effect on people. Or demons. Whatever. Somehow I knew she wouldn't give me away.

"What is it?"

"After we finished the other day…" I paused. Not knowing where to begin.

"I know."

"Huh?"

"I watched you from the edge of the trees. I wish I could say I was surprised, but I wasn't. I was more surprised that you had the foresight to keep your ability to yourself. I was going to mention it earlier, but I respected your right to privacy. In fact, I would counsel you to keep doing just that."

"Really?"

"Yes. You already remind the others a little too much of another Fallen, to add to that might not be wise."

"But it doesn't bother you?"

She laughed again, this time it felt more natural, like she was getting used to it. "Not in the slightest. I knew the Usurper very well. While you two might be akin in power, you couldn't be more apart in disposition."

I sat down on the closest rock. "What was he like?"

"Arrogant. Headstrong. Willful, Prideful, and a host of deadly other things. His intentions might have been noble, but his reasoning behind it became warped and twisted, just like we have become. You on the other-hand. You are shy. Inquisitive. Caring. No, young one. You do not remind me of him in the slightest. I trust the power that lies within you is much safer for all of the realms than it was within him."

"And you're not worried that I might become twisted?"

"Not in the slightest. You have too many people around you who care about you deeply, who will guide you, nurture you, and scold you when you screw up!"

She had no idea. Even my enemies seemed to take great pleasure in the scolding. "Thanks, Raven."

"You are more than welcome."

I pulled my scooter into my driveway just as the sun set, plunging my little world into the soft glow of twilight. I smiled as I slid off the seat, no longer in pain. My shitty day had turned out okay.

Caelyn opened the door to the kitchen almost as if she had been waiting for me to get home. I think that might have been the most uncharacteristic thing she had ever done. It set a sense of dread shivering down my spine.

"What's wrong?"

She looked at me curiously. "Why do you think something's wrong?"

I pulled my cell phone out of my pocket and hit the home button. No alerts popped up on the screen, so I didn't miss any calls or texts, so maybe there was no emergency. "You're waiting for me…"

"No I wasn't. Mom told me to take out the trash, but then I saw you were already out here."

"Hahaha. Very funny. Brat."

She gave me the usual grin she had when she made a funny. Usually at my expense. "Just kidding. I saw you pull up while I was raiding the fridge. I heard about the blow up at school. Just checking to make sure you were alright. Are you alright?"

"Better actually. Things turned out okay."

"Jessie still hate you?"

"No. She apologized and we made up right after it happened."

"Good. She's the best thing that has ever happened to you. I'd hate to see you lose her because you were stupid."

"Hey, that's not very nice. Or true," I said as I walked up the steps and into the kitchen, Caelyn closing the door behind me. "It wasn't even my fault."

"Yes it was. Never call a girl crazy, even when they are. First rule of living a longer life."

"When did you get so smart and how the hell did you know I used the word crazy?"

"I asked Claire. She could hear your whole conversation."

"Nice," I said and opened the fridge. "What's for dinner?"

"We ate meatloaf. Mom left you a plate in the microwave."

"Meatloaf!" I punched in two minutes on the keypad and hit start on our ancient microwave without even looking at the contents.

"Stop!"

I hit stop and spun on my sister. "What?"

"Mom covered it in tinfoil. Take it off before you set fire to the house, dumbass."

"Oh. You scared me. I woulda saw the sparks. No need to yell."

Unfortunately the damage was already done. Mom came running into the kitchen. "What?"

"He hit start on the microwave without taking the tinfoil off."

"Connor. Look before you think."

"Huh?"

Mom sighed realizing she wasn't making much sense, at least to me. "Just pay attention to things around you," she clarified and went back to wherever she was before she decided to impart her words of confusing wisdom upon my fragile head.

I shrugged and popped the door open, reached in and removed the tinfoil before hitting start.

I leaned against the counter as my food spun, merrily zapping my dinner with flavor-giving heat and radiation. I happened to glance over at my sister who seemed to be waiting patiently for me at the kitchen table. Something was on her mind and she wasn't spilling it. Nervousness replaced hunger.

Instead of just asking her, I waited patiently for my food, grabbed it and some silverware, and sat down across from her. I sprinkled a bunch of salt on without tasting it. Most people would yell at me for this, but I knew my mom's cooking. She never used salt. I took a bite and let it melt on my tongue. Very few things could make me as happy as Mom's meatloaf.

"What's on your mind, Cae?"

"Huh?"

"Come on. You were by the door when I got home, you waited for me to heat up dinner, and now you're sitting with me while I eat. Either you want something or you want to talk about something. I'm all yours. Which is it?"

She sighed heavily. I could see her trying to bolster her confidence and just spit it out. "It's– Hell, I don't even know how to start."

"How about the beginning?"

"Yeah. It's just taking that first plunge. Give me a minute."

I nodded and started in on my dinner a little more earnestly. After a few mouthfuls, the silence started getting to me. I had no idea what could be bothering her unless it had to do with something vampiric. "Is it fang related?"

"Kind of."

"You know I'm no expert. Is this something you should be talking to Elizabeth about? Unless it's about Jenny?"

She shook her head. "No."

"Cae, you know you can ask me anything."

"I need your help."

"With?"

"I don't want to be a vampire anymore."

It didn't surprise me. Truly, I wished I could wave a magic wand and make it all better, make it the way it used to be, but it wasn't possible. I thought Cae understood that. "You know there's nothing I can do, right? That's not how it works. Trust me. I tried. I tried to give Jessie her sight back months ago."

"I know. I had a little talk about things other than you with Clarisse."

My stomach knotted. "What exactly did you two talk about?" I already knew what had been said. I could feel hope coming off my sister in waves.

"On how the Fallen's magic works. On the price of having your wishes granted…"

"No. Absolutely not. Trust me. Learn from my mistakes. *Nothing* is worth the price of your soul. Don't you think I would go back and undo what I did in heartbeat if I could?"

"But you won! You got to keep your soul. I talked to Clarisse about what happens when you die. What happened to

Jenny when *she* died. What exactly is the difference? I get to be human again and the Fallen get my soul when I die."

"No. Absofrigginlutely not!"

"It's a price I'm willing to pay."

"It's *not* what I'm willing to pay. Cae, I will fight with *everything* I have to keep you safe and your soul yours. Don't argue with me on this, I won't give in."

"It's *my* decision."

I could feel the anger well up inside me. Caelyn slid her chair away from the table. She looked ready to fight. "No, Cae. It is not," I said and stood up from the table, leaving the rest of my meal untouched.

"Don't walk away from me!"

She was around the table and blocking my way in the blink of an eye. Maybe a half a blink. I tried to ignore and walk around her, but her hands gripped my arms. It became a problem when I felt her talons start to pierce my flesh.

"That hurts," I said calmly and pulled her hand off my left arm.

She looked down at her hands and gave a little gasp. "Connor…"

"What?"

"I'm wearing my orb."

Sean Hayden

Chapter 19

I sat back down at the table. Cae stared at her hand incredulously. I reached up, took it, and pulled her down into the chair next to mine. "Cae, your powers are…for lack of a better word, extraordinary. I have the same problem. When they first turned me into one of the Fallen, I wore an orb. Then my power started leaking through. I don't know if you're going to be able to wear it for much longer."

"What happens then?"

"We'll find you a nice cave in the middle of nowhere, and maybe throw a sofa and a TV in there for you."

She stared at me for a moment or two before she realized I was only kidding. "Now is *not* the time to joke."

I sighed, reached over, and brushed a stray lock of hair out of her face. "I know. But laughing beats crying."

"Is it that bad?"

"No. I don't care what it takes. We'll figure a way through this and find a solution to your problem."

"You mean a *different* solution than I've already come up with," she said in an exasperated voice.

"Yes. Caelyn, you're my sister. I can't let you sell your soul. No matter how much easier it would make things. All I ask is for a little time."

"For what?"

"To find a solution that will make you happy, and keep your soul in your possession. Deal?"

She thought about it a moment, which was a big step up from stubbornly saying no. "Deal. But I also want you to promise me that if you can't find one, we go with plan A."

"Maybe," I said with a wink. "I promise I will think about it. Can I ask you one more question?"

"Yes?"

"Is it that bad?"

"What?"

"Being a vampire. Do you absolutely hate it?"

She thought about it before speaking. "No. I mean I spend most of the time being human, thanks to the orb. *But* I didn't ask for it. I didn't wish for it. It was kind of thrust on me and *that* makes me feel dirty. Does that make sense?"

I nodded. "Gotcha."

"It does have its downsides though."

"What?"

"Feeding. Even with the orb, I can feel the hunger for blood always there, nagging at me. It's like being hungry twenty-four seven. That and feeding is… Let's just say it's uncomfortable."

"Taste yucky?"

"No. Too good. It's unbelievable. The bad part is… Nevermind. Not discussing it with my brother." She actually blushed which only confused me more.

"What?"

"Let's just say it's *very* pleasant. For both people. And while Elizabeth is a great friend, that amount of pleasant with another girl is *uncomfortable.*"

I gulped and nodded in understanding. I also decided I didn't want to hear any more about it. Ever. "So. How about the Phillies. Think they'll go all the way this year?"

"Did you just change the subject to baseball?"

"Yes. Yes, I did."

"Good."

We both laughed and it eased the tension in the room about a million percent. I stood up, ruffled her hair, and fell to the ground.

I could hear Cae call my name and the sound of her chair as she slid it back to stand up, but the room around me vanished into a swirl of light that faded into darkness.

Suddenly, I was standing between two trees at the border of the park by the library across town. I recognized it from the time I had spent there when I was younger. It still had the same tornado slide and ancient swing set. I watched a young couple by the swings. She sat in the blue plastic swing, while he stood behind her, gently pushing her while they talked. I could feel the fire in my belly as hunger washed over me.

I couldn't take it anymore. In a fit, I had thrown away the orb the stupid demons had given me to hide what I was, but I wanted to be a vampire. I didn't want to hide. Especially from the cattle that surrounded me. I was above them. They were food.

The demon's warning kept me in check for the longest time. For months I had been a true vampire. Sleeping during the daylight hours and feasting on blood at night. I hunted deer in the woods around my home, but I knew what I wanted. I wanted to drink from a human. I wanted to feel their hot blood wash down my throat as I drank the life from them. I wanted to drain somebody dry. Just once. Just to know the power, the feeling. I wanted to be a real vampire...

I gasped and came-to looking at my sister, leaning over me worriedly. "I have to go. *Now!"*

I sprang to my feet and ran out the door into the backyard. Ignoring Caelyn's frantic pleas from behind me, I leapt into the air, called my wings, and flew frantically toward the library. I knew I didn't have much time. I could feel the hunger overwhelming the rationality in the vampire's mind.

The last time it happened, I instantly knew everything about the soul I was about to reap. This one had been different. There was *only* hunger. It was as if it had consumed him from the inside out already. There wasn't anything left but the driving need to feed. I pitied the poor teens in the park, trapped with the monster they didn't know was there.

In desperation, I beat my wings faster.

I landed in a cloud of dust by the swings. The couple wasn't there. I remembered the angle which the vampire had stared and gazed in the direction I knew he had been just a short while ago. Nothing. Then I heard the scream from the parking lot next to the ancient library.

Another burst of speed and I was in the middle of a bloodbath. The girl had fallen to the pavement and was scrambling to get away from the grisly scene before her. The vampire had claimed his first human victim: her boyfriend.

The vampire had sunk its fangs into his throat. Blood splashed the car door he had been trying to open for her. The vampire let the body go and it slumped to the ground. I almost became transfixed as I watched the poor boy's soul leave and start to drift upward. The vampire's hiss brought me back to the task at hand.

As he turned to claim his next meal, I ran and swung my fist while putting myself between him and the screaming girl sprawled on the ground. The bones in his face crunched as my fist connected. Pain lanced upward from my hand, but dissipated and healed by the time I stopped and spun.

Fear appeared in the vampire's eyes as realization of what and who I was dawned on him.

"Shit," he spat, and ran instead of fighting.

I looked behind me at the girl. "Don't call 911 and wait here," I said as I mind magicked her into complying. I took off after *my* prey.

He ran straight through the park and headed toward the woods he had come from, hoping to lose me in the darkness beyond. Little did he know, I could see him perfectly, just as I could see the streak of blond heading toward him from the east. It collided with him and they both tumbled across the mulch covered playground.

When Caelyn sank her fangs into him, he screamed and then stilled as whatever sensations a vampire's bite of Caelyn's breed did to overload his system. I slowed and walked up to them.

Before I could speak, Cae pulled away, licked the blood from her lips, and tossed his head to the ground. He wasn't dead, but he would be soon. I looked at my sister as I kneeled down next to the fallen monster.

"What did he do?"

"He killed a guy over by the library. I wasn't fast enough to stop him." I felt the weight of guilt settle in my chest. "I saved his girlfriend. It was the best I could do."

"You can't save everybody, Connor. All you can do is try."

I nodded and put my hand on his forehead. His skin was cold and clammy. I assumed it was from the lack of blood. I used my power to reach inside him to find that spark that was his soul and pulled. It took only a moment and the blue light that was usually present was very dim and faded in and out of view. Without any words or remorse, I let it go and didn't watch it as it flew up and faded into the night sky.

"Thanks for your help, Cae. You might want to go home while I deal with the rest."

"No. I don't mind helping you."

I thought about arguing, but just nodded. She had seen the worst, the part I hated. Now it was just cleanup.

When we made it back to the parking lot I realized one thing, I had no idea what to do with a human body. The vampire had crumbled to dust as soon as his soul left, but the human was still there and bleeding. So was the girl. She stared straight ahead, not paying attention to her surroundings as she remained under the effects of my mind magic. I decided to deal with her first.

I knelt in front of her and lifted her face to look straight into her eyes. "What's your boyfriend's name?"

"Jimmy."

"You and Jimmy came to the park tonight. He told you he had someplace to go and something to take care of and wasn't sure if he was ever coming back again. He was very sorry, and hated that he had to hurt you by leaving, but he didn't want you to get involved."

"That was nice of him."

"Wasn't it? Jimmy was a good guy, and you will miss him, but it's for the best."

"Definitely."

I helped her to her feet. "Go on and head home and get some sleep. You'll feel much better in the morning."

"Good night," she said and wandered off, leaving my wide-eyed sister and the corpse of her boyfriend as my only company.

"That was *totally* cool."

"No, Cae. It wasn't. How would you feel if somebody messed with your mind like I just did to her?"

"That's the catch. I wouldn't know. And you did your best to make it right."

I nodded, not caring anymore. I just wanted to deal with the body and go home. "True."

I stood over Jimmy. Or what was left of him anyhow. His throat was mess of shredded flesh. If I left the body, someone might chalk it up to a bear attack, but they might run DNA tests on the wound anyway. I couldn't take the chance. I just didn't have a clue how to deal with it.

I thought about fire, but I had no idea how long it would take to turn the body to ash, or if it would even work. With my luck there would be a charred skeleton left for the librarians to find in the morning. I had never seen Darius deal with one either. Everybody had always ushered me away when they cleaned up my messes.

A nagging thought trickled its way into my brain. It often happened that way with being a Fallen. Sometimes, knowledge would just make its way in there. A vision of my sword answered my question.

Without thinking about it, I called my blades and sank them deep into Jimmy's flesh. Immediately, the wounds began to smoke and sizzle as fire spread out and consumed him.

Weapons that had been created to harm the Chosen evaporated humans in a heartbeat. Convenient.

When there was nothing left of Jimmy, I turned to my sister, who looked like she was going to be very ill at any moment.

"Not what you had in mind, huh?"

"No. But I'm glad I saw it."

"I'm glad you did, too. Now you know what it means to lose your soul and how fragile it is to be human. Now you know why I don't want you to make a deal with the demons."

She nodded and dropped it. "Can we go home now?"

"Hell yeah."

Chapter 20

After the longest day in recorded history and the worst night's sleep since the dawn of time, I felt like going back to school about as much as I wanted to get the word "anus" tattooed on my forehead. My alarm sounded like a death knell.

Mom barging into my room and telling me to get my lazy butt out of bed didn't exactly enhance my mood either. She took one look at my face and said, "What's wrong."

I'll admit it. I used my powers for evil. I looked her straight in the eye, let out a little bit of magic, and coerced her into calling the school and telling them I was ill and wouldn't be in today.

With a blank look on her face and a smile on her lips, she went to do just that. I buried my head under the pillows and sighed heavily. Then my conscious got the better of me.

No, I didn't go to school, I picked up my phone and texted Jess that I wasn't feeling good and was staying home. *Then* I went back to sleep.

I woke up after noon, yawned, and stretched. The extra rest had done me some good. Sure, I still felt guilty about the death of the human and the reaping of the soul, but I no longer felt like I needed therapy to deal with it. Who said sleep wasn't magical?

My growling stomach reminded me that I'd never finished my dinner from last night. I pulled myself from the warmth of my bed and padded downstairs in my boxer shorts. Mom was at work, Dad was at work, and Caelyn was stuck at school. I had the house to myself. More importantly, I had the house and my Playstation to myself. I saw a couple of sandwiches, a bag of chips, and a twelve-pack of Mountain Dew on the menu.

I took the stairs two at a time and landed just as a knock sounded on our ancient wood front door. Briefly, I debated ignoring it. After all, I was a minor, home alone. Mommy always said never to answer the door for strangers. With that reasoning firmly lodged into my head, I turned toward the kitchen instead of the door.

The knocking grew louder as I rummaged through the fridge looking for lunchmeat. By the time I got the pound of roast beef out and the bread out of the breadbox, I couldn't take it anymore. I set everything down on the counter and walked quickly to the front door with every intention of giving whoever was knocking a solid piece of my mind.

Forgetting what I was wearing, I reached out, grabbed the handle, and pulled the door fully open. Clarisse stood there looking rather annoyed. "What the hell, you can't open a door?"

"Sorry. I figured you were a Jehova Witness or something. What are you doing here?"

"Came to check on you. Your sister was rather worried."

"Oh. I'm fine. Rough day and night. Come on in." I backed up, let her in, and closed the door behind her. "I'm making a sandwich. Want one?"

"Sure," she said and followed me into the kitchen. I picked up the bread and threw together some lunch for us.

"How come you're not in school?" I set the plate of two sandwiches, a pile of Doritos, and the can of Mountain Dew in front of her. She immediately dove in.

"Didn't feel like being there. And I told your sister I'd check on you."

"Weird. She could have just texted me."

"She said she did. You didn't answer."

I reached down for my phone and realized I was standing there in my boxers. "Um. I'm going to go get my phone. And put some clothes on. I'll be right back."

"Your food will get cold. Eat first."

"It *is* cold."

"It will get warm then. Sit. Eat." She pushed the chair out with her foot. I felt rather uncomfortable, but sat down next to her anyway. "So, other than the explosion at lunch, what else happened?"

"Had to reap a soul last night. Nasty vampire. He killed a human before I got there."

Clarisse set her sandwich down, reached out her hand, and put it on my arm. The warmth of her skin sent a prickle of goosebumps up my arm. "You can't always save everybody. The quicker you learn that, the quicker you'll fall into your roll."

"I know. I tried. I saved his girlfriend at least."

"You dealt with the body and cleanup?"

"Yeah. Nobody told me how to deal with a human body, but I figured it out on my own. Thanks."

"Sorry. Not a Reaper. I forget what you do and don't know."

I nodded at her apology. I still wasn't in the greatest of moods and didn't want to take it out on her. Especially when she could still kick my ass. "No worries. You working tonight?"

"No. I actually have the day off."

"Cool. You're welcome to stay here, but I might not be the best company."

"I'll stay," she said with a funny lilt in her voice.

I started picking at my food, lost in thought. Clarisse and I fell into a comfortable silence. She finished eating before I did and took her plate into the kitchen. I was staring out the window and nibbling on my food when she walked up behind me. She put her hands on my shoulders and just stood there while I replayed everything from last night over and over in my head. She knew I was brooding and just comforted me.

"You okay," she asked when I finally set my food down, uninterested. It sucked. I had woken up refreshed and at peace with what happened, but now it was all I could think about.

"Yeah. I'll be fine."

"I didn't ask if you would be, I asked if you were. That tells me you're not. Want to talk about it?"

"Not really."

"Want to forget about it?"

"Definitely."

"Call of Duty?"

"You bet your ass. I'm player one though!"

I stood, tossed my food in the garbage and my plate in the sink, and took off upstairs leaving Clarisse standing in the kitchen. As soon as I was back in my room, I kicked the door shut and grabbed some shorts, boxers, and a T-shirt out of my dresser. I figured she would knock before she came in, so I pulled off the old boxers and scrambled to get the new ones on. I had them over one foot when the door opened.

I froze.

"I brought more Dew…

"I uh…"

"Am naked…"

"Changing."

"Your door has a lock!"

"No. It doesn't."

"Oh."

We were frozen. She wasn't turning away. I wasn't getting dressed. I don't think either of us knew what to do. I did notice that her eyes were glued to me, but not on my face. Finally she gasped and turned around. I quickly pulled up my boxers. "Sorry. Sorry. Sorry," was all I could manage to say.

"My fault. I didn't know your door didn't lock. I should have knocked."

"I should have changed in the bathroom. Didn't think about it. Sorry you saw me naked."

She laughed. "Yeah. It was horrible. Are you dressed?"

"Yes. Boxers at least. Let me get my shorts on."

She turned around anyway and sat on my bed. I wasn't totally sure, but it looked like her cheeks were a little redder than usual. "It's your house. You don't have to put shorts on if you don't want to. We're just playing video games."

"I um… Yeah. I think I better."

"Up to you," she said disinterestedly.

I pulled my running shorts up over my boxers and felt a million times safer. For some reason. I don't know why.

I turned the console on, grabbed the two remotes from the charger, and flopped down next to her on the bed. She yanked one from my hand and propped some pillows up at the other end. I liked to lie down when I played, but I guess she didn't. She kicked off her shoes and brought her legs up on the bed, stretching them out next to my head as we waited for it to finish turning on. The logo flashed on the screen and then the COD logo finally appeared with the start screen.

"Set it up. I'll be right back," she said and slid off the bed.

"Where you going?"

"Getting rid of my jeans. I'll be right back."

"Um. Clarisse?"

"Yeah?"

"Nevermind."

She opened the door and walked into the hallway. Thank the Creator. For a moment I thought she was going to just pull off her jeans in the middle of my room. We were friends, close friends, but not *that* close.

The bathroom door opened and she came back into the room, lightly closing the door behind her. I was afraid to look, so I chose the players and the map. I hit start as I felt her sit down next to me on the bed and pick up her controller.

Bare legs and feet stretched out next to me. I looked out of the corner of my eyes at her toes. I think it might have been the first time I had ever seen her without shoes. I was half-expecting talons, but she had dainty feet and cute toes with a pink, perfectly manicured little nail on each one. I gulped as my eyes travelled over the smooth skin of her legs. I stopped at her knees and turned toward the TV, not wanting to look any higher.

Okay. I did want to, but I didn't.

The game started and she sniped me in the first twenty seconds. It was a clean headshot, too. I groaned while I waited to re-spawn.

"Ha!" She nudged me with her leg, bringing the warm skin against my shoulder. I had put shorts on. Maybe I should have put a shirt on, too. Long sleeves. Maybe a hoodie.

I re-spawned back in the middle of the ship where I had started. I tried sneaking to where she had sniped me from a different direction, but she was waiting for me there. I rounded the corner into a well-placed knife attack to the face. I lowered my head in humiliation.

"Oh, come on. It's not that bad." She patted me on the back. With her foot.

"Says the girl with a two kill streak one minute into the game."

"You just need to accept my superiority. Tell you what. I'll only use my knife for the rest of the game."

"You just stabbed me in the face."

"True. But at least I won't be able to snipe you with it."

Ten minutes later, Clarisse was dying of laughter and I had only killed her once. "I hate you."

"Awww. But I wuv you. And I wuv killing you! Want another Dew?"

"Sure."

She got off the bed and I turned to watch her leave. Her jeans were gone. She had put on shorts from somewhere. If you could call them that. They were dark grey yoga shorts with the word "smoking" stenciled across the back of them in big pink letters. They ended about a half an inch above her butt, leaving the bottom of her cheeks hanging out for the world to see. And by world I mean me. I gulped and turned back to the game. I had brought up the start screen to choose a different map. It was the farthest thing from my mind.

I valued Clarisse's friendship more than anything next to my relationship with Jess. For the five-thousandth time I wished that Clarisse was a little less attractive than she was.

I loaded the map and waited for her to come back before starting the round. She did and I made the mistake of looking up. The shorts looked even better from the front. I shook my head and focused on the screen.

Instead of taking her original position, she set her can of soda on the floor and handed me mine, split and then plopped down and lay the same direction as me, putting her face to face and shoulder to shoulder with me. "Hit start."

I did.

The second round didn't go any better than the first. I managed to kill her twice, but she utterly wrecked me. At the end, she leaned over and... Well I hope she had meant to kiss me on the cheek, but I happened to turn at that exact moment in time. Her lips landed on mine.

It started out innocently. I should have pulled away. She should have pulled away, but we didn't. I felt her lean into the kiss and I turned on my side. Clarisse scooted closer and brought her arm over me, slipping her hand over my shoulder and down my back. I rolled even farther, drawing her across my shoulder and onto my chest.

Her lips parted and I felt her tongue brush across my lips. I opened my mouth and the kiss truly started. She climbed on top of me, never pulling her mouth from mine. My hands lifted and slid down her back and over her butt. I grabbed two handfuls and she moaned into the kiss.

"Connor. Jess is downstairs, I told her I would see if you were up. I see that you are. Claire, could I talk to you for a moment?"

No kiss in the history of mankind had ever ended so abruptly. My sister's voice from my door dripped with anger and disdain. My life was–for lack of a better word–over.

Clarisse slid off me, looking more embarrassed than I had ever seen her. She was quiet, too. Another uncharacteristic trait.

Cae turned and stopped. "Jess doesn't know Claire is here. I'm not going to say anything. Ever. We'll talk later. Claire and I will be in my room, talking. Take your girlfriend to the mall, Connor. Go somewhere. Far."

I nodded, even knowing she couldn't see me since she was facing my open door. I threw on a shirt and walked downstairs in a daze.

Sean Hayden

Chapter 21

"Hi Jess!" I tried to sound more excited than I felt. It wasn't that I wasn't excited to see her, because I was. It was the pit of fear and guilt that had swallowed my stomach that made me not feel it like I should.

"Are you okay? I texted you like twenty times and you never answered!" She ran up to me and wrapped me in her arms as soon as I cleared the bottom step.

"Yeah. I just slept most of the day and now I can't find my phone."

"As long as you're okay," she said and squeezed me a little harder, but then her arms went rigid. She turned her face into my chest. I thought she was going to start crying, but she inhaled. Deeply.

She pulled away and looked at me quizzically before reaching up and grabbing my shirt, pulling it to her nose. She sniffed again and again. "Why do you smell like perfume?"

"Cae just gave me a hug."

"No. Your sister wears Dolce & Gabanna. I know. I gave it to her. You smell like..." She sniffed again. "Sunflowers," she said and I could see the gears turning in her brain.

She looked up into my face and must have saw a little bit of guilt. Without a word, she pushed me away and walked up the stairs. I followed. She opened my door first. She sniffed the air, frowned, and looked around. Then she went to my sister's room.

Without knocking, she opened the door. I closed my eyes, and waited for the killing blow. I didn't hear an angry scream, so I opened them back up. My sister was lying on her bed, earbuds on, and mp3 player playing God knows what. She pulled one bud out and asked, "Everything okay?"

Unconvinced, Jess walked into my sister's room. She looked around and sniffed the air. "Was anybody else in here?"

"No?"

"Sorry, Cae. I thought I heard a voice."

Jess looked mortified. "I'm not feeling that well," she said to me. "I think I'm going to head home."

"Are you sure you're okay?" I hated the game I was playing, but... At that moment in time, it wasn't guilt that drove me. What Clarisse and I had done was inexcusable and would *never* happen again as long as I lived. I was truly grateful my sister had come up at that exact moment and put an end to it. But that wasn't my driving motivation right then. It was not hurting Jess. If she had found out about it... I was actually worried about her. She looked hurt, confused, and a little unwell.

On the verge of shaking, she nodded. "Yeah. I think so."

"Want me to drive you home?"

"Do you promise me nobody was here?"

"Of course," I said and tried to sound convincing.

She nodded. "No. I'll be fine. I think I'll have a quick nap and call you when I get up."

I leaned in and pressed my lips against her forehead. "I hope I didn't get you sick," I said. I even went so far as to press my hand against her forehead to feel her temperature. That seemed to mollify her and she slumped against me.

"I'm sorry. I didn't mean to sound like an accusing bitch. I thought I really did smell a different perfume. That and I've been worried sick about you all day. Hurry up and find your phone so I can call you later." She let go, kissed me softly on the lips, and left Cae's room.

"I'll walk you out," I said and followed, not daring to look at my sister.

I opened the front door for her and kissed her again. "You sure you don't want a ride home? You can pick your car up later if you want."

"No. I'm okay now. I really don't know what came over me. I think I was still sick over what happened yesterday. It's okay, Connor. Love you. I'll call you in a bit."

She kissed me one more time and left. I closed the door gently behind her, turned, planted my back against it, and slid to the floor. The urge to vomit almost overwhelmed me.

Clarisse and Cae came down the stairs.

Neither one of them looked happy, but Cae looked *pissed.* "Sit down, both of you."

Clarisse took a seat on the couch. I stayed on the floor. I really didn't feel like moving. "I'm sorry." I said the words, but I don't know who I was saying them to. My sister who caught us, the friend on the couch that I should have shown a little more restraint with, or the girl that I loved who had just left and had no chance of hearing me. I guess it didn't really matter. I was sorry to all of them.

"Yes. You are. Sorry is definitely a word I would use to describe your ass right now. What the hell, you two? I thought you were just 'friends' and that nothing could ever happen between the two of you. Trust me. If Jess weren't completely in love with my moron of a brother, I would be happy for you two, but come on!"

Clarisse looked even guiltier. "It's my fault."

"No. It's both of your faults," Cae replied.

I nodded. "It is. She leaned over to kiss me on the cheek to say sorry for beating me. Fate intervened and I happened to turn at the wrong moment. Our lips locked."

"Don't hand me the bullshit. That kiss was no cosmic accident. *You* weren't wearing a shirt and *you* barely had any damn pants on." She even pointed at each of us in turn. "Let me ask you this. What would have happened if I hadn't walked in at that *exact* second? Would you still be up there?"

"No!" We both said it at the same time, but I looked at her and she at me. We both were questioning our response.

"Right?" I tried to get some affirmation from her.

"Of course not. I'm not into worms. That kiss was a total accident. In fact, I think it made me a little sick. I'm going home to take a shower and gargle with some bleach. He still tastes like pretzels."

Clarisse stood and I watched her go. Grateful, actually, that she was leaving. "Wait," I said and she turned back, looking hopeful. "Where's your car? Why didn't Jess notice it in the driveway?"

"It's still at school. I flew here. Rule number one with skipping, always leave evidence that you didn't," she said, turned, and strode out the front door, slamming it behind her.

196

I looked over at my sister, who looked like she wanted to do very harmful things to me right at that moment. I opened my mouth to say something, but she just held up her hand for silence.

"Talk to me when you grow up and stop thinking with your boy-parts."

Needing to blow off some steam, work out some aggression, and basically get my mind off of things, I decided to go meet with Raven. That and I was afraid of missing a session with her. She might hurt me.

The clearing was empty as I stopped my scooter between the last of the trees. At least she couldn't swoop down from above and cleave me in half through the dense branches and leaves. At least I hoped she couldn't. Warily I looked up while I got off and walked the rest of the way into the clearing.

I made my way to the center when she finally made her appearance. There was no attack. She simply walked out from the trees on the other side and met me in the middle. I could tell by her face that something was wrong. She looked less happier than usual.

"What's wrong?"

"I need to leave," she said simply.

I nodded. "Oh. Okay. Is everything alright?"

She shook her head. "Unfortunately, no. There's been more incidents in the areas surrounding."

"What kind of incidents?"

"Like the one involving your sister. Changed humans have been attacked and killed. Reaped for no reason. Whoever is behind it is breaking our laws and must be found. The Covenant has been in place for eons. The Changed must be protected."

I nodded in understanding, though I was confused why Raven would be helping. She usually avoided the duties of the fallen. "What about my sister? And her friend? Should I be worried?"

"Yes. Keep watch over them. Should you find anything... Call me."

"How? I didn't know you had a cell phone."

She rolled her eyes in exasperation. "Simply think of me and call my name."

"Oh." I did understand. I had used the ability to contact Clarisse in the past. I didn't know it would work with any of the Fallen. I guess that's how Clarisse called Darius when she needed him.

"Connor. Be careful," she said and turned to leave.

"Raven?" She stopped and turned to look at me over her shoulder. "Thank you. For everything you taught me."

"Our training isn't over yet! I wish to dance with you again, youngling. Take care for now."

I nodded, gave her a small smile, and waved as she left me standing alone in the center of my clearing. I sighed and headed back toward my scooter. With little else to do, I had only one other thing that could cheer me up... A bag of pretzels.

Chapter 22

Raven's warning about my sister nagged at me on the ride to the mall. I decided to play it safe and called her cell. It went to voicemail. I was pretty sure she was still pissed at me and ignoring me, but I had to be sure.

I drove past the mall and headed to the house to check on her. The front door was locked, my parents weren't home, but Cae was. She was in her usual position, listening to music on her bed.

Even with her music blaring at dangerous levels, she heard me enter her room. "What?"

"Want to go get a pretzel?"

She pulled the earbuds from her head and gave me a level look. "Look. I don't know if you know this, but you're not my favorite person in the universe right now. So no."

Okay. I deserved that. "I know. But I'm feeling like shit and hoping a pretzel will cheer me up."

"So go."

"But I'm also worried about you. And Elizabeth."

She scrunched her eyes in confusion. "Why?"

"There's been more attacks. It wasn't just you. I just found out."

"Am I in danger?"

"You could be. It's why I don't want you alone. Will you come get a pretzel with me?"

"Okay," she said and I heard a tinge of fear in her voice.

"Call Elizabeth. Let her know what's going on and tell her to meet us there."

I left her room to let her get dressed and make the call. Changing my shirt quickly, I headed downstairs to wait for Cae. The doorbell caught me off guard and I almost stumbled down the last few steps.

I crept as quietly as I could to the front door and peered out the peephole. The last person on earth I wanted to see was standing there, the last of the day's sunset casting an orange glow on her normally blond hair. I sighed and opened the door.

"What?"

"I couldn't stand it anymore. I had to come and apologize."

"Shannon. Just do me a favor. Don't look at me, don't talk to me, and more importantly, don't ever touch me when Jess is around."

She seemed angered at first, but then an evil smile slithered across her face. "So does that mean I can touch you when she's not around?" Without waiting for an answer, she ran her fingertip from my neck down across my stomach and only stopped when I grabbed her wrist.

"What has gotten into you? Why are you doing this?"

"I want you. I want you more than anybody I have ever met."

"But I'm taken. I'm in love with Jessica."

"For now, but that doesn't mean you will live happily ever after. If you want me to wait, I will."

Okay, I was totally creeped out. "Um. Okay. Yeah. You go wait. Over there," I said and pointed east.

"I knew you would want me to wait. Don't make me wait too long. I'm not a patient person."

She shot an evil glance over my shoulder and left. I breathed a sigh of relief. That Chosen was bat-shit crazy.

"What was that all about?" My sister's voice from behind me made me jump.

"Your guess is as good as mine. She's not right in the head."

"I gathered that by your conversation."

"You heard all that, huh?"

"Dog ears. Comes with the fangs."

"Yeah. I know. And don't you mean bat ears?"

She punched me in the arm. "Let's wait inside. Elizabeth is picking us up so we don't have to ride the scootermobile."

"What, you don't like the scooter?"

"It's fine for one person, but have you ever ridden behind you? Your cologne smells like rotten moose."

"It's called eau de Cae. I thought you might like it."

"Har har," she said and sat down on the couch to wait.

"Does it really smell bad?"

"Not like rotting moose, but you could find something better." I was about to fall into the recliner when I saw Elizabeth pull into the driveway with her SUV.

"Come on, let's go."

Cae called shotgun and hopped in the front, which was fine with me. I liked Elizabeth and I missed Jenny, but alone in the backseat was good. I figured as much distance between me and any other girl besides Jess was a good idea.

"Are we really in danger?"

Elizabeth's question caught me off guard. "Honestly, I don't know. What I do know is that I'm not willing to take the risk. You're far safer with me than by yourselves."

They both nodded at me. Cae looked a little doubtful, but I let it go.

"So why the mall?"

"I wanted a pretzel. I've had a bad day."

"Pretzels are like antidepressants to him. I think they even help with his ADHD and cleared up his acne," Cae explained.

"Sometimes I miss having acne," Elizabeth said. Cae gave her a strange look.

"Why on earth would you miss that?"

"Because it meant being human."

"That I get. I'd practically do anything to be human again," she said and gave me a dirty look.

I rolled my eyes and stared out the window in silence for the rest of the drive. I was not going to debate the merits of not selling one's soul again with my sister. I may have promised her I would think about it, but I lied about other things, too.

We pulled into a very crowded mall. I groaned at how busy it was. I still needed to figure out what to get Jess. I didn't have clue number one.

Elizabeth didn't have the blessing of the parking gods like I did and we ended up almost as far as you could possibly park while still being on the mall property. I debated calling my wings and flying to the freaking entrance, but my sister would probably make me carry her, too. So I walked.

The smell of freshly baked pretzels wafted over us as soon as we opened the door. I started salivating. Ditching the two vamps with me, I made a beeline for the rapidly expanding line. I just hoped they saved some for me.

Pretzels in hand, I looked around for my sister. They were nowhere in sight. I almost panicked, but figured they were safe enough in the mall. It was obscenely crowded. Hard to kill a vamp without people around you getting suspicious.

I sent a quick text to my sister to have her call me when they were ready to go, slipped my phone in my pocket, and headed toward the Gamestop. I hadn't been there in ages and I had no idea if any new games were coming out that were worth my time, and more importantly, my money.

I weaved through the crowds and past endless clothing, shoe, and jewelry stores. Finally, the red and white illuminated Gamestop sign came into view. It didn't even look that busy.

The smells of plastic, stale food, and unwashed teenagers assaulted my nose as I crossed the tile to carpet threshold. I blinked a few times and looked at the new release posters behind the counter.

"Hey, Connor."

"Jeremy? When did you start working here," I asked with a smile and walked up to him. We bro-fisted and grinned. Yes, we were those guys.

"My uncle closed his garage. I had to find suitable employment elsewhere. I got lucky and ended up here about three weeks ago."

"Sweet. Anything new coming out that I should be interested in?"

"Wolfenstein. Pre-order it now."

"I'll grab a twenty from my folks and do it tomorrow. I'm broke."

"You need a job."

"Are they hiring?"

"Hahahaha. You funneh man. You have to wait 'til someone dies or grows up to get a job in this place."

"How did you get one?"

"They recognize the talent when they see it. That and my mom is dating the manager."

"Ewww."

"Big time."

"Well, if anybody looks sick or on the verge of getting a corporate job and family, let me know."

"Here. Fill out an application. At least it will be on file. I'll let Ray know you're looking."

"Thanks," I said and started filling out the paperwork. It was only one sheet, front and back, thank the Creator.

"How's everything else been with you? I hardly ever see you anymore."

"I know. I'm sorry. Between Jessica and Claire, I don't get to hang out much. Basically it's same shit different day."

"I hear ya. I'm working tomorrow. Drop by with the pre-order. I can give you the employee discount."

"Thanks, man," I said and handed the application back to him. It was a little bare between my lack of school experience, work experience, and life experience. They didn't even have a column for soul sucking demons. The bastards. "Gonna go wander. Don't work too hard."

"Not gonna happen."

I walked out the front, narrowly missing a collision with a smoothie wielding gothic wannabe. "Watch–" She started to yell at me, stopped midsentence, blushed and hurried around me. I had never seen the girl before in my life, so I didn't have a clue.

The big name stores were at the other end of the mall. My sister and Elizabeth were probably in there drooling over the latest fashions. I rolled my eyes. Clothes and I had a love hate relationship. My mother loved to buy them for me and I hated wearing them. It's not like I had a love for running around naked, I just didn't care what they looked like as long as they covered the important parts. Yes, I was a fashion nightmare.

Lately even Jess had started buying me clothes now that she could see what I wore. Every once in a while she'd hand me a bag. At least she made an effort to buy me stuff with video game logos, or Doctor Who stuff on them. I looked down and smiled at the Tardis on my chest. And then I noticed how small the shirt was getting and sighed. I definitely was filling out.

I shrugged and headed for the food court. I wasn't hungry, but I could go for a coffee. Maybe I'd even try one of the foamy ones. They made them out of soy milk or almond milk. I knew that for a fact, Jess drank them like water.

I walked past Angelique's Closet with a cringe before I remembered Clarisse wasn't working. I let out a breath of relief. I still didn't want to think about today and seeing her wouldn't help. Even walking by her store brought a flash of lips and the warmth of her skin to the forefront of my brain. I felt a blush creep onto my cheeks as I hurried past and headed toward coffee.

Surprisingly enough, even with the mall as busy as it was, the food court was somewhat deserted. It was still busy, but not compared to the rest of the mall. I must have hit a lull.

I got into line at Starbucks behind two giggling girls that were a year or two younger than I was. They kept glancing back at me. I tried my best to ignore them when someone bumped into me from behind. I turned around and Clarisse was there. I groaned inwardly and tried not to let my disappointment show. She might punch me.

"I thought you weren't working tonight?"

"I'm not, but I was bored."

"You want a coffee?"

"No. I just like standing in random Starbucks lines."

"Haha." I could feel a cold sweat starting to break out on my face. I was about two seconds from starting to shake. "What kind of coffee do you want?"

"Verona. Black."

It took about ten minutes for the line to clear to the point where we could place our order. I pulled out my remaining cash and handed it to the barista. "My treat," I said to Clarisse.

"Thank you," she said with a half-smile.

We stood, somewhat closely, while we waited for our caffeine. You could cut the tension between us with a chainsaw. I knew the moment we had our drinks and sat down, that we were going to have a conversation I didn't want to have. I handed the black steaming cup of coffee to Clarisse, grabbed mine, and motioned toward some empty tables off to our right.

We sat and we stared at each other, waiting for the other to start talking. She broke down first. "Connor, we need to talk."

I couldn't help it. I started laughing. "Sorry," I said.

"What's so funny?"

"The whole 'we need to talk' line. No shit, Clarisse. We definitely need to talk. The problem is that I *don't* want to. Would it be too much to ask to just forget it?"

"Could you?"

"Probably not until the day I die."

"That's the problem. Neither could I."

That took me a little by surprise. "What?"

The blush that crept up on her cheeks was almost cute. Definitely hot, but cute, too. "Look. Maybe you're right. Maybe we should just drop it and pretend it never happened."

I groaned, put my face in my hands, and started shaking my head. "What is with every single girl I know?"

"What?"

"Jess blows up at me, Shannon stops by the house today to tell me she'll wait for me? And you, you're confusing the hell out of me. I think my brain is going to explode."

"Say that again?"

"My brain–"

"No. The other part."

"You're–"

"Nope. Before that."

I saw where she was going with it. "Yeah. Psycho Shanria stops by my house to tell me she likes me and that she'll wait for me and Jess to break up. Oh, and to hurry up."

"I swear I'm going to kill that bitch."

"Tell me about it. At least Jess wasn't there for *that*."

"I'm just grateful your sister came up first. Did she read you the riot act?"

"You don't even want to know."

"I don't have to. She pretty much let me have it, but in a sisterly kind of way. I know you can't stand her, but I kinda like the twerp."

"She's growing on me, too, now that she's not a stuck-up cheerleader bitch."

"I'm surprised she let you out of the house," she said with a little giggle.

"She didn't I dragged her and Elizabeth here to keep them safe."

"From what?"

I realized she had no idea what was going on. "I went to train with Raven this afternoon. She left."

"To go where? I thought she was supposed to be training you?"

"Whoever attacked my sister and killed Jenny is still out there and it's attacking even more of the Changed. I guess there's been a few attacks in the surrounding cities."

"When did this happen?"

"I don't know. Raven said I should keep an eye on my sister and Elizabeth."

"What about the other Changed?"

"What others?"

"Connor, there are a couple dozen of them in Cedar Creek alone…"

"Oh. Shit. I don't know."

"I'll be right back. I'm going to contact Darius. Stay here."

"Say hi to Dad for me," I said with a grin.

"Not funny. Don't move."

I watched her run out the food court entrance and into the brightly lit parking lot. I sipped at my coffee and watching the people around me when my phone started ringing. I pulled it out of my pocket and Jess' face was on the screen.

"Hi, baby," I said when I answered it.

"Hi." She sounded better but still a little down.

"How you feeling?"

"Better. What are you doing? Want to come over?"

"I'm at the mall with the brat and one of her friends, want to come up here?"

"Okay. I'll be there shortly. Where will you be?"

"I'm in the food court sipping Starbucks and missing you."

That earned me a little giggle. "I'll be there shortly."

"Hey. Pssssst. Guess what."

"What?"

"I love you."

"I love you, too."

She hung up and I shoved my phone back into my pocket. Clarisse came in with a worried look on her face. "I contacted Darius."

"And?"

"They're on their own. They're searching for whoever is doing it, but can't guard everybody."

"What should we do?"

"Keep the ones closest to us safe," she said and nodded toward Cae and Elizabeth, who were walking toward us. My sister didn't look too happy to see Clarisse.

"You guys didn't buy everything in sight?" I tried to keep my voice cheerful sounding.

"No. Hi Claire," my sister said and leveled her gaze at her.

"Hiya, kiddo. Just discussing the game plan to keep you two safe. So far we've come up with strength in numbers, public places, and not letting you out of our sight."

We did? Sometimes I was in awe at how smoothly Clarisse could spout out the bullshit. "Yeah."

"I also contacted the head of the Reapers. They are all out searching for whoever is doing this. Don't worry. They'll catch him."

That seemed to mollify both the vampires. "Jess called, she's on her way up here, so if we have anything else related to this, we need to get it over with now."

Everybody turned and gave me a dirty look. Well, Elizabeth didn't, but Cae and Clarisse did.

"Good," my sister said with a sneer that rather worried me.

"Yeah. Smooth move, asshat. Your sister told me," Elizabeth said and punched me in the arm.

"Guys. It was all my fault. Leave your brother out of it."

The two girls turned and looked at Clarisse. "Huh?" They did the unison.

For the first time since I met her, Clarisse looked fragile. "I said it's not his fault. I kissed him."

"Why on earth would you kiss *him*?" My sister actually sounded disgusted.

Clarisse shot her an angry glare. "Look, Cae. I don't know how to tell you this. I know he's your brother. I know you have a certain image of him, but… Your brother is hot."

"Yeah right."

"Seriously. Close your eyes. Turn toward him and open them quickly."

Cae did exactly as she was told. For the first time in her life. "I still don't see it. He looks like Connor to me."

"He looks like Connor because he changed in front of you slowly, day by day. Look at his arms. Look at his chest. He's twice the size he used to be. Look at his hair."

"Whatever," my sister said and looked to her friend who was nodding emphatically. "Ewww. You, too?"

Elizabeth shrugged and said, "Not interested, but he is hot. You've got your brother filters on."

I was blushing. I could literally feel the heat pouring from my face. "Okay, guys. Enough."

They all turned and looked at me and started laughing.

"What did I miss?" We all turned to Jess with a steaming cup of Starbucks in her hand.

"We're going to go underwear shopping and were laughing at your brother's discomfort. Do you want to go with us or hang with the worm here?" Again, Clarisse flabbergasted me. She should quit being a demon and be a spy.

"I'll take the worm. Thanks though," she said with a smile.

Sean Hayden

Chapter 23

"Want to go for a ride?"

Jessie looked more like herself than she had in quite a while. I smiled at her and gave her a quick peck on her lips. "Where to? Not that it matters, I'd go anywhere with you."

"I don't know. It seems like all we do is go to the mall. I was thinking maybe the park?"

"Good plan," I said and stood, offering her my hand to help her up. She took it and it felt good to touch her again. "One sec, I'll text Cae I'm leaving and have her catch a ride with Claire or Elizabeth."

I pulled out my phone and did just that, leaving another note to stay with Claire until I met up with them later. Slipping it back into my pocket, I offered Jess my arm. "Well, aren't you the gentleman tonight."

"Gasp! Should I ever be ungentlemanly around my lady, please, striketh me down."

She giggled and took it and we headed out into the parking lot. "I'm sorry about earlier today," she whispered and squeezed my hand.

Guilt washed over me again. If anybody owed anybody an apology it was me. Unfortunately it was one that would never come. I did the next best thing. "No you don't. Ever. I love you. If you're ever sick or whatever, I'll always be there for you."

"I love you, too," she said and hit the unlock button on her key fob.

Her mustang blinked and beeped merrily a few cars away. I followed her to the driver's door and opened it for her, closing it softly once she was inside. I blew out the breath I had been holding in, swore I would never kiss anybody again as long as I lived, and walked around the car. She reached across the car and popped the door open for me. With a smile, I slid in.

"Thanks."

"You're welcome. It was the best I could do without getting out of the car, walking around, and holding the door open for you," she said.

"You're such a gentleman," I replied with a wink.

She started the car and backed out of the spot. "It's nice to be alone with you. It feels like it's been forever."

"It has. So. Whatcha wanna do at the park?" I wiggled my eyebrows while I asked.

"Swing on the swings?"

"I can do that," I said and gave her a quick kiss as she put it into drive and took off. "Hey, lady. Keep it under forty. We're in a parking lot."

"Nervous Nellie."

"Woman driver."

"Least I can!" She laughed and had a point.

"Wanna take me to get my license this week?"

"Absolutely. Don't you have to work?"

"No. I got laid off."

"Awww. Who was it? I'll set the building on fire for you?"

"Hahaha. It's not a biggie. I have enough money socked away for your present," I lied.

"What is it?"

"Not gonna tell you. You'll have to guess."

She thought about it for a few minutes on the drive to the park. "I give up. I can't think of anything. Unless it's jewelry, which I don't wear, so if you waste money on sparkly stuff I shall have to swat you."

"Nope."

"Good. I guess you'll just have to surprise me then."

"Okay. I will." *I'll surprise me, too.*

We were at the park within ten minutes. We chatted the whole way and Jess even took one of her hands off the steering wheel to hold my hand. That made up for the week I had been having. I missed her and for some strange reason I felt like I just got *my* Jess back. I lifted her hand to my lips and kissed it as we pulled into the park.

She parked and we got out and headed toward the playground together, laughing like a couple of little kids. "Push me?"

She ran toward the swings. Sitting down, she waited for me to catch up. I walked up behind her, gave her a little kiss on her neck, and pushed.

She wobbled for the first few pushes, but then we both fell into the rhythm. "Not too high!"

"I won't," I said with a laugh. "What are you doing this weekend?"

"I don't know. I hadn't thought about it. Got anything in mind?"

"How about if we go to the park. Then we could go to the park. Maybe top it off with a trip to the park?"

"Sounds like the perfect weekend," she said and I could hear the smile in her voice.

I felt the sudden, unavoidable urge to hold her. On her backward swing, instead of pushing her, I caught her in my arms. "Gotcha," I whispered into her ear.

"Whatcha gonna do to me?"

"Hmmm. Maybe kiss you?"

"Oh, yeah? Well… You gotta catch me!"

She pried herself loose and bolted toward the tornado slide and jungle gym. I cheated. I full on used my powers of good for evil nefarious purposes. I caught the woman I loved in my arms and carried her to the slide.

"Hey! You cheated," she said with a pout.

I kissed her. "How did I cheat?"

"You used rocket boosters or something."

I looked down at my feet and behind my back. "Nope. I forgot to bring them with us. That was pure talent, baby."

"Oh. Okay then. You may kiss me some more then."

I did as she asked and leaned forward, pushing her back against the cool metal of the slide. I knelt down in the mulch in front of her and wrapped her in my arms.

She tasted sweet like strawberries and hotter than the sun. I could feel her melt beneath me as her lips opened to mine. The only sounds around us were the crickets and the soft moans that escaped from Jess. They drove me on. My hands slid down from her face, over her shoulders, and onto her chest. I cupped her for the first time.

I expected a moan of protest and for her to push me away, but she didn't. She reached down and unzipped her hoodie, allowing me even more access. I broke our kiss in surprise.

"It's okay," she whispered and reached up, pulling me back in for more kissing.

I slid my hands back over her chest and squeezed gently. Her soft moans turned into one long gasp of pleasure. She bit my lip, none too gently, either. It was my turn to moan. Her tongue invaded my mouth and her fingers dug into my back.

I pulled away long enough to whisper, "I love you."

"I love you, too."

Reaching up, she pushed me back, but she didn't stop there. She kept pushing until I fell backwards onto the mulch. Smiling, she slid off the side and straddled my hips on the ground. It was her turn to be in control.

She grabbed my hands and put them on her hips as she leaned in again, her mouth finding mine. She kissed me like she had *never* kissed me before. Still full of love, it was also filled with wanting and urgency. While she kissed me, she started grinding her hips against me…

"Oh, my God," I groaned into her lips.

"Yes," she whispered and continued.

She started panting into the kiss. Finally her lips just rested against mine as she fought to breathe, the passion between us intensifying even more.

I was going crazy with want and I could barely stand it. Jess sat up and continued. She looked down at me with all the love in the world and with glowing green eyes. Glowing in the darkness of the night. Glowing… *Oh, shit.*

She called out my name, arched her back, and two white feathery wings erupted from behind her.

She screamed and fell to my chest, passed out cold.

I lifted Jess and got her into her car. She lay nestled into the passenger seat still unconscious and wrapped in her wings. I had to physically restrain myself from reaching out and touching them, they were that soft.

Nervously, I got behind the wheel of her mustang. I had never driven a car before, but I couldn't see it being harder than a scooter. Or so I kept telling myself.

I buckled up and pulled my cell from my pocket, dialing her dad after I backed up out of the spot. He answered on the third ring.

"Hello?"

"Hi, Mr. James. It's Connor."

"What happened?"

"She had a little accident."

"I'm on my way!"

"No. Stay there. I put her in her car and am driving there."

"I'm confused. I assumed you meant with her car?"

"No, sir. She… I don't even know what to say. Her eyes started glowing and she sprouted wings, sir. She changed."

"Oh. I see. I'm glad you were there then. May I speak to her? Is she afraid?"

"She passed out, sir."

"Thank you, Connor. I'll see you shortly," he said. "Call me again if she wakes up before you get here. I'll calm her down."

As luck would have it. She did wake up as soon as we pulled into her driveway. She opened her eyes, saw her wings, and screamed again.

"Jess! Look at me. You're going to be fine. I promise. We're back at your house. I called your dad. He will explain everything! Jess!"

Her screams turned into sobs as she looked at me with wide frightened eyes. She started hyperventilating. "It's okay, baby," I kept repeating over and over while we slowed to a stop.

"I'm… I'm… I'm a freak. Why are you not screaming?"

"Because you're my angel," I said softly.

That seemed to help. I could see her visibly relax as she looked down at the feathers around her. She even reached out her hand and gave it a tentative touch.

Mr. James was standing on the porch waiting. I half expected him to have his wings out, but he didn't. He looked like his normal self. He ran to Jess' door and pulled it open.

"Daddy," she said as her voice started trembling again.

"It's okay, sweetie. Daddy will explain everything. Come inside."

He reached in and pulled her into his arms, lifting her like the little girl she would always be to him.

"I'm scared," she whispered.

"You have nothing to be frightened of. I'll explain in a moment." He turned to me and gave me a sad look. I offered him a reassuring smile. "Would you care to join us, Connor?"

"If you want me to, sir."

"It involves you as well. Come on." He turned and carried her up to the porch. I walked around him and opened the door for him.

He entered the house and set Jess down on the couch. I stood behind him, not wanting to be in the way. "What's going on? How does this involve Connor? What the hell am I?"

"We sweetie. Us. All of us. Even Connor. And it involves him because he saved your life and tried his best to give you a shot at being human. Apparently your body picked the stronger route."

He walked over to the mini-bar he had set up in the living room and pulled out three glasses and poured some amber colored liquid into each of them. My parents drank, so I knew it was whiskey of some sort. Probably scotch by the fancy crystal bottle it was in. He picked up all three glasses in one hand, gave one to me and Jess, and sat in the chair across from her. He took a small sip.

I did the same and shuddered at the taste. Jessie stared at hers and then back at her dad. "Go ahead, sweetie. You will never be able to get drunk, but it does have a calming effect on one's self. Or so I learned over the years."

"I'm confused. Are you trying to tell me that you're like me?"

Mr. James nodded and stood. With a soft *thwump* he called his wings. They weren't as pristine white as his daughters, but they were still majestic. "I am."

"What about Mommy?"

"Unfortunately no. Your mother was a beautiful human being and yet more angelic than the best of us."

"Connor?" She looked at me with pleading eyes.

I looked at Mr. James who shook his head slightly. *Not yet.* I could read it in his face. "I'm not human either, but I'm not the same as you and your dad."

She looked terribly confused. "I don't understand."

"Welcome to our world, sweetie," he said and sat back and began his tale. He told her of the creation of the earth and the angels. He told her about the war and the split between the Chosen and the Fallen and their different views of the world. He didn't sound angry or bitter, nor did he highly embellish the Chosen's role in the war like I half expected him to.

Mr. James sat in silence for a moment and let it all sink in before he continued with his tale of how he met her mother and fell in love and the disaster it always brought to the offspring of such a pairing. My heart broke as I heard him describe how he had loved her mother and how overjoyed he was when Jess came into the world and then it shattered when he told her of her mother's loss. No matter the bad blood between Chosen and Fallen, no man should have to go through what he did when he lost his love.

The rest of the tale Jess knew from experience. Waking in the hospital and all that. What she didn't know was my role. When Mr. James began explaining that there were more creatures in the world than Chosen and Fallen, I took over the tale and explained about Brett and how he had been created by a Fallen in exchange for his soul, how he had gotten out of control and almost killed her.

"So where do you fit in?" She looked at me confusedly. "And more importantly, what are *you*?" She asked the question, but I think she already knew the answer.

"I used to be human," I said and stole one more glance at her father, who nodded his approval this time. "But then one day, I got the idea to sell my soul for my fondest wish… I thought it was a joke and I thought I was just goofing around until one of the Fallen showed up to grant my wish."

"What happened?"

Sean Hayden

"Well. In an effort to outsmart them and keep my soul, I did something stupid."

Mr. James gave a short bark of laughter. "And incredibly brave," he said.

"What?" Jessica looked intrigued.

"I wished to become one of the Fallen."

"You two are making all this up. And it's not funny."

"Says the girl with angel wings," I said to soften the mood.

She glanced behind her and gave them a little wiggle and shrugged. "So let's see *yours.*" She looked at me.

Fear ran through me like a chill. This was the moment of truth. She would either accept me or not. There was little I could do but hope for the very best. "Okay, but I'll be honest, they're not beautiful like yours."

I called them and they came. Jess' eyes rounded. "I *remember*," she said. "I remember you saving me, and you too, Daddy. You said I was hallucinating!" She looked at me accusingly.

I shrugged and held up my hands innocently.

"I told him to. He was under strict instructions from me," her father added helpfully. "I didn't know if you would stay human or not, and I didn't want to burden you if you were."

"I *sooo* wouldn't use the word burden. You kept things from me, the both of you. Not happy." She crossed her arms for emphasis. "But I do understand," she said and stood, first crossing the room to hug her father and then she crossed to me. She reached out and gently stroked the leathery membrane between the bones of my wing, sending a chill down my spine.

"I actually think these suit you a little more than the fluffy ones, you little devil."

I gave her a smile and went to hug her. She backed up a step and my heart froze, but I nodded. "Okay. I'll let you two talk about the rest." I said trying my hardest not to let my voice catch. If it did, I knew I would break down crying and I really didn't want to do that right now. Later, when I was alone, maybe. "Have a good night, Mr. James. Call me later if you want, Jess."

I turned and walked to the door, pulling it open and stepping outside.

"Connor, wait," Jess called and stepped outside with me, pulling the door closed behind her.

I turned and my chest tightened while I waited for her to deliver the blow. "What's up?"

"Don't what's up me. I saw your face when I stepped back. I didn't mean to, but it's a lot to wrap my…um…wings around," she said and smiled at her own joke. "Don't think anything has changed between us because it hasn't. And don't think I don't love you because I do." She stepped closer and pulled me into her arms, her wings striking a beautiful contrast against mine.

"I love you, too," I said and held her tight.

"I just found out that my boyfriend isn't human. I just found out that *I'm* not human. It's a little much to process."

"I know, baby. No worries. Go ask your dad how to banish your wings. They're a bitch to sleep in."

She laughed. "I will. Does this mean we're mortal enemies now?"

"I won't give a shit if you won't."

"Not even a little bit. They can keep their war."

223

"Exactly."

"Anything else I should know?"

"Claire's real name is Clarisse and she's one of the Fallen, too. That's why we hang out so much. She is in charge of teaching me all the Falleny stuff I need to know."

"Oh. That's actually a good thing."

"Why?"

"It's much better than the whole 'we're just friends' thing."

"Ahh. That makes sense."

"Anything else?"

"My sister's a vampire?"

"Will you stop picking on her? She's a nice kid."

"Not joking. She died when you were in the hospital from a vampire bite. She woke up on the morgue table with fangs. Oh, and her friend Elizabeth is one, too, but she sold her soul for it."

"Okay. I'm going to bed now. If there's anything else, write it down and tell me later."

"One more thing."

"Your parents are werewolves?"

"No. You look damn hot as an angel," I said with a wink and kissed her one more time.

Chapter 24

I stepped off the porch and flapped my wings. I gave one more quick wave to Jess as she watched me fly for the first time. I could see her smile.

"You are sooo teaching me how to do that in the morning," she called out, turned around, and went back inside. I imagined she and her father would be up most of the night talking. I told her to call me if she needed me.

I cleared the trees next to her house and headed home, figuring Cae and Elizabeth would be there. I pulled my phone out of my pocket and noticed a missed call from Cae. I was a little nervous playing with my phone while flying, but I checked my text messages anyway.

There weren't any, so I called Cae back. It rang with no answer. I hung up when I got her voicemail.

I called Clarisse to see if she was still with them. She answered on the first ring. "What's up?"

"Just left Jessie's. She turned tonight. Wings and everything."

There was a moment of silence on the other end. Finally she asked, "How did that go?"

"Better than expected. She's having a long talk with her father right now."

"Did you show her yours?"

"My what?"

"Wings, pervert. Did you show her your wings and tell her what *you* were."

"Yeah. Her dad and I gave her the whole rundown."

"She doesn't hate you?"

"Nope."

"Give it time. She will," she said and laughed to let me know she was joking.

"Where's Cae?"

"We were all hungry after the mall closed so we're at Denny's eating breakfast. You in?"

"I used the last of my money at the mall."

"I got you. Come on. The one on Highway One."

"Be there in five," I said and hung up. I turned more north and could see the lights of the highway in the distance. I swear I could smell the pancakes. My stomach growled in anticipation.

I landed behind Denny's in the shadows, quickly dispelling my wings. A cat jumped out of the dumpster and scared the hell out of me. "Stupid cat."

I found the three of them sitting in a corner booth. I couldn't believe how packed the place was, but then again, nothing topped off Christmas shopping like a twenty thousand calorie breakfast.

Clarisse scooted in and made room for me. Cae shot us a dirty look. I shook my head at her, telling her not to worry about the proximity of our seating arrangement. I told myself it would make it easier on the waitress if we sat next to each other since she was paying.

"So. Jess knows *everything* now, huh?"

"For the most part," I replied to my sister, not falling for her baited trap to make me feel even *more* guilty than I already did.

"And she's cool with you being a little demonic when she's the angel in the relationship?"

"Opposites attract. Are you done?" I was starting to get a little pissed at her attitude.

She nodded and started picking at her omelet.

"I ordered for you. I hope you like pancakes and bacon," Clarisse tried to inject a little less hostility into the conversation.

"Perfect. Thanks."

"I told her what your favorite was," Cae added.

"Thanks."

"Well, I figured she didn't know you well enough to guess what your favorite food was. I mean, I know you two are close, but I didn't think the topic of breakfast had ever come up. Has it?"

"Cae. Enough." Elizabeth added, apparently having enough as well.

My sister *harrumphed*, crossed her arms and refused to even pick at her food anymore. I looked over at Clarisse to see how she was handling the situation. She was just staring in awe at the cattiness of my sister.

"Sister, dearest, may I speak to you outside for a moment?" I left little room for her to disagree.

"Fine," she said and rose from the table, bolting for the front of the restaurant before I even got up.

"Brat. Excuse me. We'll be right back."

"Connor," Clarisse said. "Go easy on her. We did screw up."

Sean Hayden

"I will," I said and gave her a brief smile.

"I don't blame you for kissing him," I heard Elizabeth mumble to Clarisse. Apparently she forgot my hearing was better than hers. So with blushing cheeks, I walked past the hostess stand and out the front door to talk to Cae. I had no idea what I was going to say, but it would have been good. If she had been there.

I looked around and saw no trace of her anywhere. "Little shit," I said pulled out my cell. I dialed her and held it to my ear, but it went straight to voicemail. "She shut off her damn phone."

I turned around and went inside. Clarisse saw me and frowned. "What happened?"

"Little shit took off." Just then the waitress finally brought my breakfast.

"What do you want to do?"

I looked at Clarisse and then at my pancakes. "Let's finish eating. If she wants to be a brat and run away, let her."

I sat down and dumped syrup on my pancakes and ignored the worried look that Elizabeth shot between Clarisse and me.

"What?"

"Bad guys ripping souls out of people like your sister and me?"

Shiiit. I sighed heavily and stabbed my fork into my pound of delicious pancakes. "You're right. Let's go find her."

I watched Clarisse toss a couple of twenties down on the table and waited for me to slide out of the booth. "Let's go."

"You take the SUV, swing by your house to see if she's there. If not, go to my house. It's the only two places she would go. Claire, you take to the air and follow Elizabeth, see if you can spot Cae. She may be fast but she's not as fast as Elizabeth driving. I'm heading straight home to look for her there."

"Okay," they both said in unison.

I walked away from the entrance and without giving a shit, called my wings and leapt into the cold night air. I could have flown straight home, but I followed the roadways, looking for my sister the entire way. Without any sign of her, I landed in my front yard, banished my wings, and entered the house.

The lights were off, my parents were asleep, and my sister wasn't in her room. Nor had she been there. She had to have gone to Elizabeth's to sulk. I walked outside to wait for Clarisse and her to show up, hopefully with my sister in tow.

When the SUV pulled up I knew something was wrong. She wasn't with them. I could tell by the look on their faces. When they saw me sitting on the front porch, they knew she wasn't home either.

Elizabeth got out first and looked *very* worried. "She's not here?"

"No. Not at your house either?"

"Obviously not. What do we do?"

"Well, she couldn't have gone far," I said.

Claire opened the SUV door. "What if she didn't run away?"

"What?"

"What if she was taken?"

I didn't know what to do, so I ran. I ran and jumped into the air and flew all the way back to Denny's. I landed in the middle of the parking lot, turned back into a human, and scoured the front, looking for *anything* to tell me where my sister had gone.

There was nothing.

A few minutes later, Clarisse and Elizabeth pulled up. Something that Cae said gave me an idea. "Cae said she could always feel where you were because she fed from you... Does that work both ways? Can you tell where she is?"

Elizabeth looked confused. "She didn't tell me that. I don't know."

"Try?"

She closed her eyes and turned in slow circles. "Apparently not?"

"Are you sure?"

"Pretty friggin' sure I have no friggin' clue where your sister is. I'm sorry. It would have been awesome, but I can't."

"Sorry. I know. Clarisse? Do you have any ideas?"

"I don't know. I'm sorry, Connor."

"Well, we're not going to solve anything sitting here. Let's go to the house and come up with a game plan."

The three of us drove back in Elizabeth's SUV. We were all quiet and understandably worried about my sister. When we pulled up into the driveway and saw her sitting on the front step, Clarisse and I jumped out before Elizabeth had it in park.

"Where the hell did you go?" I'll admit. I probably could have started the conversation a little more calmly.

"Home."

"We were here, you weren't. We've been looking everywhere for you!"

"I walked slowly? What's the big deal?"

I fell to my knees and sucked in a great big breath of air. Relief that my sister was okay flooded my body. I felt like passing out.

"You scared the hell out of us, Cae," Clarisse said from behind me. "We thought you were taken."

"Why didn't you answer your cell?" I chimed in, too.

"It's dead. And shit, I'm sorry. I didn't think of that. I just got really pissed off and wanted some time alone."

"Alone is fine, just make sure you're with us," I said and stood. I know she hated it, but I walked over to her and gave her a hug. "Don't scare me like that again. Please. I lost you once and I don't want to do it again."

"I won't. Promise," she said and actually returned the hug.

"Can we go to sleep now? We do have school in the morning," Elizabeth said from her SUV.

Sean Hayden

Chapter 25

I groaned as I passed through the doors of school. I moaned as I walked to my locker. Luckily, Jessie was standing there or I might have collapsed in utter dismay.

"Hey, handsome," she said with her usual early morning chipper smile. It was one of the few things I couldn't stand about her. Mornings were meant to be slept through, damn it.

"Hi, beautiful. I don't suppose you have a cup of coffee in your pocket for me?"

"Um, no. I did *have* one, but it spilled. Good thing I was wearing Khaki pants."

I laughed and gave her a good morning kiss after searching the hallways for lurking teachers. "It's the thought that counts. Thank you."

"Will you two stop sweetening up the hallways? It's gross," my sister said as she passed us, making gagging noises.

"Stop looking!"

"Come on, we're gonna be late," Jess said and pulled on my jacket sleeve.

We settled into homeroom just as the bell rang. The class quieted down with assistive shouts from our teacher. Mrs. Jacoby took her place at the podium and looked out over the small sea of faces sitting before her. Something in the back caught her eye and she gave a brief nod.

"Class, we're getting a new student today. Charles, come up here and introduce yourself."

He swished as he walked up the aisle. I caught a flash of corduroy out of the corner of my eye and looked up to see a very tall blond kid walk by. Without any hesitation, he took the offered podium and smiled out at each of us, catching as many eyes as he could, until his eyes met Jessica's. The smile that crept onto his face turned my curiosity into instant dislike.

"Hi, I'm Charles. Willoughby. My family and I just moved here from Los Angeles. Don't ask me why, I'm still not quite sure. Not that Cedar Hills isn't lovely, it's just not LA. It's nice to meet you all," he finished, flashed one more smile at my girlfriend, and walked back to his seat in the back.

I looked over at Jess, who had turned to follow his movements. She had a curious look on her face until he sat down. She gave him a small smile and turned to look at me.

"Love you," she whispered and turned her attention back on Mrs. Jacoby.

Veins started popping out on my forehead, my vision darkened, and I screamed as I ripped the desk in front of me neatly in half. Okay, none of that happened, but my eye twitched as I fought down the jealous monster welling up from inside me.

Thankfully, the bell for first period rang. I stood, as close to Jess as inhumanly possible, and waited for her to pack up her things. For the first time in my life, I was actually looking forward to algebra.

"You okay?"

I turned and looked at a bemused Jessica walking alongside me, with the barest of smiles on her lips. "Of course. Why would you ask?"

"Well. That was the first time I've ever seen you jealous before. And all over a pretty blond head, smiling at little ole me."

"I wasn't jealous."

"Liar."

"Maybe a little."

"It was hot."

"Okay, I was very jealous and I thought about ripping his face off."

"And now you know how *I* feel ninety percent of my day." She patted me on the head, and walked ahead of me to class.

"Well, damn," I whispered and caught up.

We settled into class and fell into an easy silence. Until Charles came in right as the bell rang. I tried to be good, I honestly did, but I looked around the nearly full room and noticed the only empty seat was on the other side of Jess. I growled.

People from three seats away turned to look at me. Jess covered her mouth and suppressed a giggle fit. She was enjoying this. Too much. Way too much.

"Class, this is Charles. He'll be joining our class for the remainder of the year. Please give him a warm welcome," Mr. Thompson called out to the class. "Take the empty seat over there."

Chuck wandered through the aisle and smiled yet once again when he saw who he would be sitting next to. "Hi," he said softly as he slid into his new seat.

"Hi. Charles, this is Connor, my boyfriend," she said and leaned back to introduce me.

I plastered on a fake smile and curled my hand into a fist to avoid flipping him the bird as I nodded in his general direction. His smile evaporated as he got a good look at me. Then he glanced at Jess, back at me, and repeated it several times before clenching his jaw and staring straight ahead.

"Wow," I whispered and lifted my eyebrows.

Jess just looked confused. With a shrug, she opened her book and paid attention to Thompson.

Halfway through class, I caught some movement out of the corner of my eye. Chuck reached over and dropped a folded piece of paper onto Jess' desk. It took him all of twenty minutes to pass her a note. A note! Who even does that anymore?

Jess covered it with her hand.

I gripped the edge of my desk and pretended not to notice. The creaking of shearing metal could be heard, if one had super-hearing, as I strained not to rip the bolts holding the desktop down. Jess unfolded the note, took one glance at it, folded it back up and handed it back to him.

Whew.

I took a chance and looked over at him. He looked even less happy than before.

The rest of the class passed rather quickly, but not quick enough for me. I kept glancing up at the clock, watching the minute hand tick by, wanting nothing more than to get away from the jerk-wad who seemed to have a thing for Jess.

Finally, the bell rang. I gathered my things slowly, not wanting to seem anxious. Jess actually finished before I did and waited for me. I looked up at her as I stood. Her face almost caused me to fall back into my chair. "What?"

"Let's go," she whispered, her face as white as new snow.

I nodded, slipped my arm through hers, and led her out into the hallway. "What's wrong?"

"He's one of them."

"Who?"

"Us. Chosen. The Council found out I'm not human anymore. They sent him to observe me."

"Is that bad?"

"It wasn't until I introduced him to my Fallen boyfriend…"

"Oh."

"Yeah."

"So what did he say?"

"He mentioned something about your lineage and that I am to accompany him to my father at the end of the school day."

"Are you?"

"Am I what?"

"Going with him?" Jealousy was replaced with anger and subtle hatred.

"I think I have to? I don't know. I'll call Daddy at lunch. See what he says. I'm a little pissed off at him, too. He didn't mention that we might be getting a representative from the council snooping around."

"Maybe he didn't know. I'm sure he would have if he did."

She nodded but didn't seem entirely convinced. "It figures."

"What does?"

"We're off for two weeks. He had to show up today."

Jess sat next to me at our usual lunch table, but instead of tearing into her salad like she normally did, she whipped out her phone and her fingers flew across the keyboard.

"Whatcha doin'?"

"Texting my father," she replied without looking up or stopping.

"Tell him I said hi."

She shot me an exasperated look. I had been shooting for making her smile. I failed miserably. She looked truly worried. "Why don't you call him?"

"I tried on the way down to lunch. He didn't answer."

She hit the send button and finally set the phone down and picked up her plastic fork. I was halfway through my second hamburger when I noticed she was just pushing the lettuce around her Styrofoam bowl.

"You should try actually eating it. I've heard that stuff is pretty good for you. Makes your wing feathers lustrous."

"Connor, I love you, but I'm not in the best of moods."

"I noticed. Just trying to make you smile."

She set down her fork with an exasperated sigh and closed her eyes. She started breathing in and out and finally put a smile on her face before turning to face me. "Thanks. And sorry."

"Don't be. You have every right to be upset. It's just my job to make you smile. That and it makes me happy."

"Shush. You're going to make me blush."

"I'm surprised you can stomach being around his filth."

We both turned to find Chuck standing behind us, tray of food in his manicured hands. "Well, if it isn't Percy Perfectpants. The asshole table is two down. I'm sure they saved you a seat."

Jess elbowed me in the ribs. "Not helping," she whispered.

"Apparently, Lady Jessica still has some human tendencies for bad boys. No worries. We'll straighten her out. Show her the proper path. Quell her urge for junk food."

"Well. Hiya, Cabriel. Long time no see," Clarisse said as she slid into the open seat across from Jess and me. "How long has it been? At least a century. I believe the last time I saw you, you were stuck on the end of my blade. Wasn't it during the California Gold Rush?" Disinterestedly, she picked up her burger and took a large bite out of it, looking up and giving him a big smile, showing a mouth full of food.

"Animals. Jessica, please accompany me elsewhere. I cannot stand to be in their presence any longer and I don't wish them to tarnish you further."

"Um… No? I have called my Dad. I'm waiting to talk to him about you. I highly suggest you leave me alone until I hear from him."

He seemed utterly confused, but turned around and walked away anyway. I resisted the urge to throw the rest of my burger at him.

As soon as he was gone, Clarisse put down her food and looked at us in all seriousness. "When did he show up?"

"This morning," we replied in unison.

"Great," she said drawing out the word.

"You know him?"

"Yeah. He's the Chosen Council's do-boy. What did he say?"

"That I am to 'accompany him after we leave this place of learning' and that he doesn't like my boyfriend."

"Yeah. He could probably smell Connor a mile away. I told him to shower more often."

Jess giggled. I gave Clarisse the bird. "What does he want?"

"Probably to indoctrinate Jess into the mindless drivel that is the teachings of the Chosen. Perfect world, blah blah blah."

"Are they all that bad?"

"Take one look at Shannon and ask me again."

"Good point," Jess replied. "What does that mean for me? I know my dad was someone big, but he won't go into detail about it. Now he has hardly anything to do with them."

"You don't know?" Clarisse looked at Jess who shook her head. She looked at me and I shrugged. I didn't have a clue either.

"Okay, you know Lucifer was the head of the rebellion?"

We both nodded. "Yeah, but everyone calls him the Usurper."

"Yes. Because he tried to usurp your father's role as the leader of all. We lost. The Chosen won, but eons later, he abdicated the throne. When he fell in love with a human…"

"Oh," Jess said simply.

Things started clicking in my brain. "That's why they call her *Lady* Jessica."

"Not as dumb as you look, worm. Good job."

"I thought the Archangel Gabriel was the ruler of the angels? I mean I never really went to church, but every book I have ever read, paints him as the head honcho?"

Clarisse looked at Jess, a little surprised. She started nodding slowly. "What's your father's name?"

"Gabriel James… You've got to be kidding me. I mean come on. My father is *that* Gabriel?" She didn't look convinced.

I felt a knot in my chest. Of all the people to end up with as a potential father-in-law…

"Yup. You're sorta royalish," Clarisse said with a grin, giving Jessie her best star-struck look.

"No. Daddy would have told–" She was silenced by the ringing of her phone. "Hello," she said as she picked up. Clarisse and I sat and waited patiently while Jess had a muted conversation with her father explaining the situation and flinging questions and accusations at him faster than I had ever heard her speak. Of course we could hear the whole conversation, but we pretended not to. Finally, she angrily hit the end button and slammed her phone down on the table, shattering the screen. The entire lunchroom turned and looked at her.

"Okay. I believe you. The good news is he said that under no circumstances was I to go anywhere with that creep. He was rather angry that they even knew I had changed."

"What's the bad news?"

"That we might be in serious trouble."

Sean Hayden

Chapter 26

The bell rang, echoing through my soul just as much as it rang through the halls and classes of James Underwood High. I looked up at the clock and had never ever been disappointed to see three o' clock. It was a new experience.

I glanced over at Jess and she looked about as happy as I did. I just needed to get her out of the school and home before Chuck found her. He had been in our homeroom and first period, he had even been around at lunch, bet neither of us had seen him since then.

Inwardly, I hoped the asshat had gotten so flustered he had gone home, or wherever the hell the self-righteous pricks went when they weren't bothering normal people. However, I sincerely doubted he *had* left. My luck just wasn't that good.

"Ready to go?"

I looked up at Jess and nodded, standing while grabbing my books. "As I'll ever be."

"So what's the plan?"

"The plan is to get you out of here and home."

"I know that, I meant how?"

"Stealthy as possible, forcibly if necessary."

"You're gonna protect me?" She smiled as she asked.

"With my dying breath, but let's hope it doesn't come to that."

"Well, Daddy should be waiting out front. Hopefully he can keep Chuckles at bay."

"So I just have to get you out the front door and into your big black limo. I feel so secret service agent."

"First of all, it's not a limo. It's a SUV. Second of all, you're pretty hot when you're all protective," she said and wrapped her arms around my waist.

"Roger," I said, putting my fingertips to my ear.

"And now you're just being a dork."

I nodded and gave her a quick kiss, scanning the hallway as soon as we left the class. There was no sign of Charles. I took her hand and headed for the stairwell. Luckily, I glanced over the banister before heading down. I caught a glimpse of his blond head coming up the stairs. I pulled Jess' hand and practically ran in the other direction. Luckily, our school had more than one stairway.

"Was he down there?"

I nodded. "Yeah."

"Plan B?"

"Plan B."

We dodged and weaved through the masses heading toward freedom from academic slavery and made it to and down the stairs without tripping, falling, or getting hurt. Nothing was more dangerous than a student stampede heading home.

We stepped off the stairs and made it into the main corridor leading to the outside world. The sunlight pouring in through the glass front of the school shined off the highly polished linoleum floor, casting rays of sunshine on the walls and ceiling, giving our route to freedom a beacon to follow.

"Looks like the coast is clear," Jess said and hurried toward the exit.

We bobbed and weaved the best we could, but the hallway was packed. We were about halfway through when everyone stopped moving. It was actually more than that. *Everything* stopped moving. It was like time had stopped. You could even see the motes of dust illuminated from the sun, stop their swirling dance through the air.

I had a bad feeling. A very bad feeling.

I looked down at Jess. She was still able to move, just as I was. We continued walking forward, stepping agilely through the immobile students.

Charles stepped off the stairs, just as we were about to pass by. He was clapping slowly. "Congratulations. You *almost* made it."

"Made what?"

"Your play for avoiding me. As you can see, though, it's not possible. Are you ready to go, Lady Jessica?"

"No," she said firmly, took my hand and tried to leave. We made it as far as the glass doors, which were quite locked.

"Neat trick," I said and tried two of the other doors. They didn't budge an inch.

"When you've lived as long as I have, you pick up a few tricks," he said snidely. "Now if you will please excuse us, we have business that doesn't concern the likes of you."

He reached for Jess.

I slapped his hand away.

The look of surprise on his face was worth it. "You dare touch me?"

"I dare kick your ass if you touch my girlfriend again. Leave. Her. Alone. She doesn't want to go with you. Ever."

"She does. She just doesn't know that she does. I merely wish to introduce her to the splendors of the Chosen. Surely you don't want to keep her heritage from her."

"She can learn from her father. Not from a snooty dick like you," I said and turned back to the door. I grabbed the handle and *pulled*. Not like I was trying to open it, like I was trying to rip it from the frame of the building. With a loud *creak* and some shattered glass, it opened. I gently nudged Jess through the door and outside.

Her dad was standing by the car, watching the exchange. He nodded at me when Jess cleared the building. I meant to walk out behind her when a hand grabbed my shoulder.

"Let her go. I will deal with her and her father later. Let *us* have a little chat about the hierarchy of things."

Jess stopped and nodded to her dad.

"Come on," she said.

"You go ahead. I'm going to have a chat with Chuck."

"Connor–"

"Go ahead, baby. I won't be long. Meet you at your house."

"Jess, come on," her father called from the student drop-off."

Jess reached into her pocket and pulled out her car keys, handing them to me. "Bring my car," she said and gave me a quick kiss. "I love you."

"I love you more," I said and the hand on my shoulder started squeezing. I could hear the popping of bone. I waited until she was safely in her father's vehicle, ignoring the pain in my shoulder and then I slowly reached up and grabbed two of the fingers digging into my flesh and jerked them as hard as I could.

Charles slammed into the back of me. Clearly he hadn't been expecting that. "You maggot," he screeched and pushed me out the door.

I stumbled on the concrete, but didn't fall. I wouldn't give him the satisfaction of knocking me down. I hoped. When all was said and done, he was still a lot more experienced than I was.

But then again, so is Raven…

I silently thanked my brain for the little bolster in confidence. I turned and smirked at Chuck. "Wow. You are a *dick*."

"What is that?"

"Something you're obviously lacking. Now listen and listen carefully, feather boy. Jess doesn't want to have anything to do with you or your kind–"

"You mean her kind?"

"Whatever. Just because she has the feathers, doesn't mean she's a self-righteous asshole like the rest of you."

"Think what you may, Fallen. The truth is we won the war. You have little say in the affairs of the Chosen."

"I do when they impact the ones that I love."

That pissed him off. With a flash of blue light, a flaming sword appeared in his hand. "You do not get to love that which you cannot have!" He struck, barely giving me time to call my blades.

As usual, I saw his eyes widen at the twin black swords nestled loosely in my hands. I needed to have T-shirts made that said, *they're not* those *swords*, or something like that.

Either way, his eyes narrowed and he approached, a little more cautiously this time.

He struck, I parried and attacked but missed, he was fast. Damn fast. But not as fast as Raven. I smiled and stepped forward, weaving my blades in the intricate dance I had learned.

Apparently he was never taught it.

It didn't mean he wasn't good, but fighting him was different than fighting Raven. He wasn't clumsy, just had a different style. He began smiling at me and attacked faster. I kept up but struggled to bat away his one sword with both of mine.

You're as fast as you can imagine yourself being...

Score two points for my brain as Raven's words echoed inside my skull. Instead of willing my hands to move, I imagined them already being there to block. It worked. Not only was I blocking his blade, but had more than ample time to attack. I returned his smile as his began to fade.

I let go of the hatred I had for him. I didn't want to kill him. That would probably complicate things beyond belief. I did however want to wipe the smirk off his face.

With the next block, I turned my blade and brought my other in a downward arc against his, close to the pommel. It smacked the blade right out of his hand. In less than I fraction of a second, I had both blades across his throat. I stopped dead in my movement. I tiny silver drop of blood escaped from his neck and settled itself on my blade.

He sighed and closed his eyes.

I banished my blades and punched him in the face.

He looked up at me from the concrete and snarled.

"It's over. Stay away from Jess," I said and walked away.

"It's only just begun," he said, but when I turned around, he was gone.

Sean Hayden

Chapter 27

I dropped off Jessie's car to her, and checked on her. Her father thanked me with a nod of approval before assuring me that he had everything under control and that Jess was quite safe with him. His eyes made me believe him. He looked furious and I was quite relieved it wasn't directed at me.

I gave Jess a quick goodbye before heading back to *la casa del* Sullivan. I called my scooter into being and took off down the road. It was official. We were on winter break. I wouldn't have to deal with the headache of school for two and a half weeks. I couldn't help but smile for the rest of the ride home.

I pulled into the driveway, parked my scooter on the side of the garage, and went inside to find an empty house. It was still pretty early. Mom and Dad wouldn't be home from work for another hour or so, and my sister was probably with Elizabeth watching a movie or painting their claws.

I had the house to myself.

My smile got even bigger.

I knew what had to be done. I ran up to my room as fast as my legs could carry me. Which, as a Fallen, was pretty damn fast. I double checked to make sure I hadn't set the carpet on fire on my way up the stairs.

Satisfied, I slipped into my room and turned on my Playstation 3. A little COD would help me relax. Unfortunately, my console picked that exact moment to start clicking...

The TV sparkled to life, but the loading screen wouldn't even come on. I reached behind the console, unplugged it and waited ten seconds before plugging it back in. It started clicking again. I started crying. Okay, not really crying, but I wanted to. The PS4 was out, but I didn't have five hundred bucks to spend on getting a new one... Or did I?

I could pull a scooter out of thin air, why couldn't I pull a PS4?

I couldn't think of a reason I couldn't. Not even a little one. I raised my hands in the air, picturing its sleek black contours, its shiny controllers and...

The front door exploded.

The whole house rattled in shock. I darted out of my room and hit the stairs, only to have them crumble beneath my feet. I dropped the last six feet to the ground in a crouch. Drywall dust and splintered wood blocked my vision. I could see the gaping hole where my front door *used* to be, but not much else.

The crunching of debris under foot was the first clue I had that I wasn't alone. I waved my hand in front of my face and finally made out a silhouette walking into the remnants of my living room. My parents were going to be *pissed*.

I stood, brushed the dust off, and met whoever had blown up my house at the crumbled remains of the broken stairwell. I half expected Charles to be standing there, but it was someone else and nobody I recognized.

He stood about two feet taller than me, wore nothing but leather, and had hair longer than Clarisse. "Excuse me? Why did you blow up my house?"

"I'm here for the vampire. Where is it?"

Usually when people showed up to my house, they wanted to kill me. The fact that someone was there for my sister was a bit of a shock. One I didn't like. "That vampire just happens to be my sister… Why do you want her?"

"She is an un-contracted soul with inhuman power. She must be dealt with."

"And you are?"

"Elrich the Chosen."

"Chosen what?"

"*Of* the Chosen."

"Who chose you?"

"Don't play games with me, Fallen. I can smell your stench from here."

"Oh. I thought that was you. All I can smell is ass."

He didn't take too kindly to that statement. His wings burst forth in a flurry of shredded leather that added to the debris littering my floor. Now he was standing in my living room wearing nothing but leather pants and boots. He looked like a Village People. A seven foot tall angry Village People.

Without warning and without me seeing him move, he wrapped his arms around me in a crushing embrace. I could hear my ribs cracking under the immense amount of pressure I was suddenly caught in. His lips, only inches from mine, cracked an evil smile. I brought my head back and smashed the smile from his face.

He dropped me as I felt his lips splatter against my forehead. Warm wet blood dripped down my face. I wiped it away and glimpsed it on my hand. Its silvery hue caught me off guard. When someone bleeds, you expect red. It's almost your reward for hurting the bad guy. Silver just isn't the same.

He wiped off his mouth and I could see his lips knitting themselves back together. We could get hurt, but it didn't last long. He called forth a spiked club. It looked like it could tenderize a whole cow with one swing. I *really* didn't want to get hit with it. Hell, I didn't even know if I could block one of his attacks. I briefly saw my swords, arms, and face shattering in my mind. I called my swords and stood my ground.

"What happened to the first blood rule? I made you bleed," I said sheepishly.

"Doesn't count when you use your forehead," he said and swung the massive mace in a downward arc.

Instead of blocking, I dodged it and swung one of my blades at his midsection. I totally wasn't expecting it to hit. I mean the guy was the Chosen's version of a vampire hunter. I expected him to be inhumanly fast. He was fast, but not fast enough.

Blood dripped from the wound I had made just under his ribs. It wasn't deep, but it still cut him. The blood fell antagonizing slow and struck the ground with a resounding chime...

That just pissed him off even more.

I ran around, dodging his wild swings, screaming, "First blood! First blood!"

"I'm here to kill a vampire. You're protecting it and keeping me from my duty. There is no first blood."

Well, shit.

I stopped running and turned and faced the behemoth. There were very few reasons I would stand and face an opponent like him. Protecting my little sister just happened to be on the list. "Fine," I said and crossed my blades in front of me.

He grinned evilly and swung his mace across, hoping to bash me off my feet and into the next county. Halfway through its arc, I ducked and stabbed him in both his knees. He dropped like a sack of boulders, clutching both wounds. His mace vanished. I stood and lowered my blades to his neck.

"Leave my sister alone."

He looked up at me and then to the blades at his throat. His eyes widened in fear. This time I was grateful for the recognition. He nodded.

"Say it."

"What?"

"That you give me your word that you will not pursue my sister and that you'll leave Cedar Hills forever."

"You have my word."

"Say it," I repeated and dug the tips of my swords into his throat.

"I'll not pursue the vampire and I will leave Cedar Hills forever."

I nodded, stood straighter, and banished my blades. "Now get out of my house."

He stood and left through the gaping hole in the front. Leaping into the air, he took off into the darkening sky. My living room had turned into a war zone. With a heavy sigh, I briefly glanced out the front to make sure no one was watching and began the arduous task of magically repairing everything before my parents got home.

My thoughts were consumed with worry. Something wasn't right. In the past few days, someone had killed one of my sister's friends, attacked my sister, come looking for my sister, and the Chosen had somehow found out my girlfriend had changed. It was like they had the Connor Channel in their cable lineup.

"Hey, honey," Mom said as she walked through the front door. I had just finished fixing the couch. She had good timing as usual.

"Hey, Mom," I said and sat down, pretending I had been straightening the cushions.

She walked past me, and headed toward the kitchen, presumably to start dinner. I took a deep breath and sank back into the couch to finally relax.

Her scream rang in my ears like the fire alarms at school.

I shot off the couch and found her standing at the bottom of the remnants of our stairs. *Shit. I forgot the stairs.*

"What the hell happened?"

"I don't know. I was walking down them and they collapsed."

"Why didn't you say anything?" I could hear the panic in her voice as she looked me over for injuries. I looked down, too. My pants were a little shredded, but other than that, I was fine.

"I forgot."

"Forgot?"

"Yeah. As in didn't remember."

"Don't get smart with me. How do you forget falling through the stairs? Are you on drugs?" She leaned forward and actually peered into my eyes.

This conversation took a turn I didn't want to deal with. I looked my mother in the eye, leaned forward and whispered, "The stairs are fine. You came home and no one is here. Go make dinner."

She blinked a few times and did just that. I could hear her in the kitchen banging pots and pans and soon enough, I could smell spaghetti sauce cooking. I quickly repaired the stairs before anybody else came home.

Sean Hayden

Chapter 28

I opened the front door and closed it like I had just come home. Mom popped her head out from the kitchen and said, "Hi, honey. How was your day?"

"Interesting. I'm gonna catch a quick nap before dinner."

"Okay, baby. Everything okay?"

"Yeah. I'm just tired."

She nodded and I ran up my newly repaired stairs. They seemed solid enough. The bright side is I seemed to have mastered the use of my magic. Raven's teachings really helped, and I didn't burn the house down fixing anything.

I opened my bedroom door, saw my comfy looking bed, and stopped dead in my tracks as my phone started ringing in my pocket. I pulled it out and swiped the screen without really looking to see who was calling.

"Connor?"

It was my sister. "Yeah?"

"Elizabeth and I are being followed."

I actually growled. This shit was getting ridiculous. "Where are you?"

"Mall, by the food court. We keep moving but don't want to leave. The place is packed."

"Good. Stay there. I'll find you. See if Clarisse is working."

"Shit, I didn't even think of that."

"Call me if she is and hang out with her. I'll be there in five."

The line went dead and she hung up without saying goodbye. I stuffed my phone in my pocket and ran back downstairs.

Mom popped her head out of the kitchen. "I thought you were taking a nap?"

"Can't. Meeting Cae at the mall."

"I want you both home for dinner."

"Don't worry. We'll be back shortly," I said as I ran out the door. I grabbed the scooter and drove to the mall as fast as the little engine would take me.

I parked and ran to the entrance, pulling it open and letting the warm air and food court smells wash over me. My stomach growled in response and I told it to shut the hell up. My phone rang again and I pulled it out of my pocket. Looking briefly at Cae's face, I answered.

"Is she working?"

"No. I'm getting a very bad feeling."

"I'm here. Head toward the food court again. I'll meet you halfway. Stay on the line."

I heard her tell Elizabeth where to go and then listened to the sounds of the mall echoing through the headset on my phone. Finally, I spotted them in front of Northern Candle Company. I nodded and hung up. I could see the relief on my sister's face when she spotted me.

"Where are they?"

"I don't know. She was behind a column by Angelique's, but disappeared when I called you."

"It was a she?"

"Yeah."

"Did you know her?"

"No. But it was definitely a woman."

I nodded and decided not to tell her about the vampire hunter who had showed up at our house. "Come on. Let's go home. Mom's making spaghetti."

"Is it safe to leave?"

"You're with me. All's good."

She gave me a brief look of disbelief, but shrugged and turned to Elizabeth. "Dinner?"

"Your mom's spaghetti? Hell yeah."

"Where did you guys park?"

"The entrance by Hot Topic," Liz answered. I nodded and let her lead the way. I figured riding home with them would be better and mentally banished my scooter.

As we walked, I let the space between us grow and moved off to the side, keeping an eye on them. Caelyn kept shooting me nervous glances but I made a walking gesture with my fingers. I wanted to see if I could spot whoever was following them.

We made it to the exit without anyone showing themselves. I was actually a little disappointed. I didn't like the idea of whoever was following my sister, still out there.

"Cae. I know I'm your icky brother, but don't go anywhere without me for a while okay?" I looked at Liz to make sure she knew that included her, too.

"Why?"

"Just trust me on this one, okay?"

She stopped dead in her tracks, put her hands on her hips, and stared me right in the eye. "What's going on?"

I took a deep breath and decided to spill it. "Someone showed up at the house today and practically destroyed it looking for you."

"Who?"

"One of the Chosen who claimed to be their vampire hunter. He didn't like the idea of an un-contracted blood sucking teenager running around town sucking the life out of everybody."

"What?"

I sighed. I'd tried to make a joke to make her smile, but she just looked totally confused. "You became a vampire without contracting your soul to get it. They no likey."

"Oh. Did you tell them they could make me human again and shut the hell up?"

The fierceness in her voice broke my heart. "If it were possible, Cae, I would have already done it."

She softened her expression. "I know. I just wish you'd let me *make* the damn contract. It's worth it to me. I wish you would get that."

"What?" Elizabeth joined the conversation, not knowing about our earlier discussion on the merits of soul selling.

"I told him I'd sell my soul to be human again. He won't let me. The big jerk."

Liz nodded in understanding. "You're being selfish."

My sister and I both turned and stared at her. My sister asked, "Which one?"

"If you want my honest answer… Both of you."

"Huh?"

"Cae. Your brother is just trying to keep you safe and that means both in this world and the next. It's why he doesn't want you to sell your soul. Connor, your sister didn't ask for this. She doesn't want to be a vampire. Hell, I don't want to be a vampire. Wishing for this was the stupidest thing I've ever done. Especially now that Jenny is gone. I feel like part of me died with her. Top that off with a big old side of 'she's being hunted *because* she's a vampire' and you've got a big mess on your hands. If she were human again, there wouldn't be a problem."

I sighed and closed my eyes. She had sort of hit the nail on the head. I nodded and looked at my sister. *Really* looked at her. "Is that what you want?"

"Yes!"

"You realize once you die, your soul will belong to the Fallen. I don't even know what that really means, but it could be bad."

"Could it be worse if I ended up with the Chosen? Could it be worse if I ended up just wandering around the universe?"

"I don't know."

"You're a Fallen. I trust you to look out for me when I die."

That made me smile. "You know I will, brat."

"Then yes. That's what I want."

"Okay. I'll talk to Clarisse."

That put a gleam in my sister's eye. "Thank you!"

"You're welcome. Let's go home. I'll call her on the way."

I turned and headed toward Liz's SUV. "Tell her that her boss is pissed off."

Without turning, I asked, "Why?"

"Because she didn't show up for work even though she was supposed to close."

I stopped moving. The world stopped turning. My heart stopped beating. "Cae…"

Cae stopped walking and looked at me. Realization hit her hard. "No. This is Claire we're talking about. She's like uber-badass. She's fine. I'm sure of it. Right?"

The more she spoke the more unsure she became. I closed my eyes and thought of Clarisse. Usually when I did that it sort of opened a link between us. All the Fallen could communicate that way. I wasn't good enough to do it yet, but I could usually see where she was and what she was doing. This time I could tell she was there, but that was it. Nothing but blackness. She was either asleep or in trouble. I sincerely doubted she would miss work to take a nap. "She's in trouble. She's alive but in trouble."

"Where?"

"I don't know. Come on. Let's go home. I'll keep trying and try to get ahold of Darius."

We piled into the Explorer and Liz gunned it toward my house. I kept trying to picture Darius in my head, but without *any* luck. He was in the realms of the Fallen. I had no idea how to contact him there. I even went so far as to try Raven. I had the same amount of luck.

By the time we were inside and seated with plates of spaghetti in front of us, I was in a near state of panic. I didn't even remember filling my plate. But then again, maybe I hadn't. Cae was looking at me worriedly. Maybe she filled it for me.

My parents were talking animatedly and Liz seemed to be doing her best to keep them occupied. I tried picturing Clarisse for the thousandth time. She seemed to be getting weaker. So did my heart.

I growled and pushed my food away from me. Standing, I left the dinner table ignoring the shouted questions from my parents. I only had one option left and I had no idea if he would even help me. I walked out the front door, ran down the street a bit, and launched myself into the air.

It took only a few minutes to fly to Jessie's. I landed in her front lawn and pounded on the door without even banishing my wings. Mr. James opened the door, took one look at me, and opened it even wider. "Come in."

"Thanks."

"What's wrong?"

"I don't even know where to start. Something's killed one of my sister's friends when it was attacking my sister, one of the Chosen's vampire hunters showed up at the house looking for my sister, my house got nearly destroyed in the process, and now Clarisse is missing. She's alive but in trouble."

"You wouldn't happen to know anything about this would you, Cabriel?"

I turned and saw the snobby bastard sitting in the big leather chair in Mr. James' living room. Jessie came skidding down the stairs. She saw me and my wings and knew something was wrong. "What is it?"

"Claire is missing."

She turned and stared at Chuck, too. All three of us stood there and watched the smug expression on his face. "No.

I did not have anything to do with the missing Fallen. Nor did any of the Chosen. That would be a breach of the accords."

"Tell that to the one whose ass I kicked after he nearly destroyed my house."

"What?"

"You heard me. He was there after my sister."

"Your sister is the rogue vampire?"

"Ha! I would hardly call my sister a rogue anything. She doesn't even want to be a vampire."

"That is of little consequence. She is an un-contracted immortal. She cannot be allowed to continue."

"She's my sister and if you touch her, I'll beat your ass back to Valhalla. Prick."

He stood and called his blade. Mr. James moved so fast I didn't even see it. He had Chuck in a one-handed grip against the wall. "Not in my house. Get out."

He physically set Charles down on the ground and dragged him to the front door by his throat. I resisted the urge to cheer. Jess wrapped her arms around me.

"Do you think she's okay?"

"She's alive, but not able to answer me. All I see is blackness."

"You can see her?"

"Only what she's doing. I haven't gotten the whole telepathy thing down yet."

Mr. James tossed the Chosen out on his front lawn and slammed the door shut. "If you can't see her, she must be unconscious."

"I figured that much. Caelyn was being stalked at the mall. She called me and I told her to find Clarisse at work. Her boss told her she never showed up. I had a bad feeling…and well you know the rest."

"Indeed," Mr. James spoke softly.

"What are you going to do?"

"I don't know. It's why I came here. I was hoping your dad would have a suggestion."

"Have you contacted Darius?"

"I…" I took a moment to blush. "I don't know how. He's in the Realms."

"Simply close your eyes and picture him in your mind's eye–"

I opened my mouth to interrupt, but he stopped me.

"I know you cannot see him. Picture him and simply call his name. He will hear your call."

"Oh," I said bashfully. I did as he said and pictured Darius in all his scary glory. I must have also been more worried about Clarisse than I thought. My worry conveyed my need to speak with Darius. I whispered his name and it came out like a clap of thunder. The walls of the James Mansion shook with the power of his name.

There was a flash of light and Darius stood in the middle of the room, looking around bewilderedly. Mr. James cleared his throat and said, "Not what I was expecting, but welcome, Darius."

Darius turned to the Chosen and bowed low. "I thought the boy called me, but thank you for inviting me into your home."

"He did call you. Or at least I told him how to call you. By the look on your face you had little choice in the calling."

"His power is...unusual. What is it, young one?"

"Clarisse has been taken."

"I'm sure you are mistaken. No one of the Chosen would take–"

"I'm afraid he is correct. Look into his mind. You will see all that has transpired as of late," Mr. James said. I was grateful for his help. They guy was kind of growing on me.

Darius strode forward and looked me in the eye. I could feel him rummaging around my head. I had the sudden urge to kick him out and throw up a mental wall. I don't know how I knew, but I did. If I didn't want him in there, he had little chance of entering uninvited. However, I wanted to save my friend. I opened up wider and let him see everything that had happened over the past few days.

I felt a certain memory of his daughter and I in my bedroom and blushed furiously. He raised an eyebrow and continued his mental interrogation.

"I see," he said simply.

"Do you know how to find her?"

"No. You did all that could be done. She is still alive so she still has purpose."

"What does that mean?"

"Whomever took her, took her for a reason. She is in no immediate danger."

"Why would they take her?"

He looked at me with a sad face. "I assume to get to you."

My heart broke. What exactly was it about me that caused people to hate me so damn much? Why was it always those around me that had to pay the price? "This blows ass."

I looked up and saw the confused look on Darius' and Mr. James' faces. "It sucks," I repeated in a more familiar phrase.

My cell phone started ringing in my pocket. Hoping for the best, I dug in and pulled it out. My sister's face was on the screen. I swiped my thumb across it and said, "Hello?"

"Do you love me?"

It wasn't my sister's voice. "Who is this?"

"Don't you recognize my voice?"

I put the phone on speaker and held it out so everybody could hear. "No. I don't recognize your voice. Who is this?"

"I'm disappointed. I thought what we shared was special…"

The flash of a kiss in the mall ricocheted across my brain. It couldn't be… "Shannon?"

"I knew you would get it!"

"Why do you have my sister's phone?"

"The more important question is why do I have your sister. Why do I have your Fallen friend? Why do I have the little vampire? Why am I going to take your girlfriend? Those are the questions you should be asking…"

"Why?" I asked the question, really wanting to know the answer. I didn't have the slightest clue. "Wait a minute. *You* killed Jenny? Why in the hell would you do that?"

"Because she saw me. She saw me when I tried to take your sister."

"Again, why are you doing this?"

"Because I love you. I know you love me, too. I could feel it in our kiss. If you didn't have all these damn women around you, I could have proved it to you. But I couldn't even get close enough to talk to you let alone prove our love."

I felt like throwing up. A lot.

I looked over at Jess and her face was as red as fire. I could tell she was about twelve nanoseconds from breaking. Her father held a comforting hand on her shoulder.

"Where are you?" I didn't think it would be that easy, but I had to ask.

"Why?"

"So I can come save my friends?"

"Wrong answer."

"So I can be with you," I held up my hand to Jess as soon as the words left my mouth and made gagging motions. And then I made crazy motions. Hopefully Jess was good at charades.

"I don't believe you."

"Oh, believe me. You felt our kiss. You were right. From the moment your lips touched mine, you're all I could think about," I said and rolled my eyes.

"If you come, you'll come alone?"

"Of course."

"You will stay and I will let the others go."

"Sounds like a good deal to me."

"Do you swear by this?"

"I do," I said without thinking. Mr. James and Darius made halting signs, but it was too late.

"Fine. I will meet you at the mall."

"But it's closed," I said.

"I will be in the center by the Winter Wonderland display."

The phone went dead.

I looked up and saw the looks of dismay. "What?"

Mr. James spoke first. "You just made a verbal contract."

"Yeah? So. I didn't really mean it."

"It doesn't matter, Connor," Darius spoke. "You promised to trade yourself for the lives of your sister and friends. You cannot back out…"

"Surely there is something he can do?" Jess looked frantic and disbelieving.

"Only through death may the contract be broken. He rushed and accepted without knowing the consequences."

"So I have to kill her or marry her?" I couldn't believe my luck. I was getting tired as shit of all the rules I didn't have a clue about.

Mr. James held up his hand. "Even though she killed. Even though she called the Council and told them of Jessie's change. Even though she set the vampire hunter upon your sister which damaged your home. Even though she has kidnapped your friends and your sister, you cannot kill her. You don't know the repercussions."

"What repercussions?"

"The end of the peace. You would start the war anew."

Sean Hayden

Chapter 29

I landed at the mall, without a plan, without a hope.

What am I going to do? What am I going to do?

The words kept repeating themselves over and over in my mind and had been since I left the James'. The image of the hurt on Jess' face when I said she couldn't come with me didn't help either. The truth was, I didn't trust Shannon. I wanted Jess safe.

The door was locked. I held my hand against the glass, pushed with a little power, and melted it. I stepped through the gaping hole I made into the quiet. It was weird being in the mall without music playing softly over the speakers. You never really noticed it while you were shopping, but the mall seemed even emptier without it.

I walked past the pretzel shop where this whole mess started and sighed. The weight of what was to come still rested heavily in my chest. It took only a few moments to reach the central raised platform of the Cedar Hills Mall. It was decorated with white flocked trees, Christmas lights, Santa's village, and every other commercial representation of Christmas you could imagine. Sitting atop Santa's throne was Shannon. At her feet were the unconscious forms of my sister, Clarisse, and Elizabeth.

I walked up the green carpeted ramp and stood before her. "I'm here. As promised."

"So I see. I almost doubted you would show up. I'm glad I don't have to kill these three, although one of them would bring me pleasure."

"You couldn't kill Clarisse even if you wanted to. Unless you want to restart the war."

"I was talking about the vampire," she said and nudged Liz with her toe. "They are the creations of your warped promises. They disgust me."

"Have you looked in a mirror lately?"

"What?"

"Nothing. I'm here. Let them go."

She stood and raised her hands. Her eyes glowed softly blue and the three of them woke from their slumber. "Leave now, before I change my mind."

The three of them shook their heads. Cae gave me a look and I motioned for her to take Liz and get the hell out of there. Clarisse, however, stood and walked to my side. She made no motion of leaving.

"Go," I whispered softly.

"I can't. You wouldn't leave me, so I'm staying."

"I apparently made a contract with this psycho. Me for you. Go."

"No. We'll figure this out. I am sooo not leaving you here with her. Alone."

"But I'm not alone."

We both looked up at her. "You mean you actually found someone dumb enough to go along with your little schemes?"

She nodded and then looked confused. "Yes."

Charles stepped out from Santa's Workshop. "You said you had nothing to do with this!"

He looked down at me rather smug. "I didn't. My *sister* did."

Well shit.

"This bitch is your *sister*?"

"You didn't know?" Clarisse sounded confused.

"No. And I can't believe you didn't tell me."

"Sorry. Forgot you wouldn't know."

I turned toward them. "So let me get this straight. Are you actually here on behalf of the Council or did you make that up, too?"

"That was true as well. My sister called and told me Lady Jessica had come into her power. When I told the Council they were ecstatic, hoping she would take her father's place. She did keep from me the fact that she was in love with a Fallen." He couldn't keep the distaste from his voice when he spoke the word Fallen. "Then I find out my sister is in love with the exact same beast. I guess it's to be expected since you're new. The taint hasn't reached your skin yet. I'm sure they both will tire of you after a few millennia. Or at least my sister will. And now Lady Jessica is free to take her place on the Council."

This just kept getting better and better. They *both* were bat-shit crazy. "What do we do?" I whispered my question to Clarisse.

"I don't know."

"You leave and Connor comes with me."

"I can't let him do that," Clarisse said forcefully.

"You don't have a choice. He made the contract."

Sean Hayden

"He could kill you. He could kill the both of you," Clarisse said deadpan, seemingly thinking about the consequences.

"And start a war? I think not," Chuck answered.

Clarisse paled. She turned to me. "Whatever you choose, I will follow. I cannot stand to think of you trapped with her for eternity. If you fight, I will fight with you."

"You'd rather start a war than see me trapped with her?"

"Yes."

I gulped. I think I needed to start accepting the fact that Clarisse wasn't just a friend. There's not too many of those that would start a heavenly war with you. I could see the tears welling up in her eyes. I reached out and wiped the start of one away with my thumb.

"Don't touch her!" Shannon's screech echoed through the mall like the scream of a banshee.

Inspiration struck. "What? You mean like this?" I leaned in and ran my hand down Clarisse's cheek. I continued on down over her shoulder and over her back. I turned as I pulled her into my arms, so Shannon could see the look of false ecstasy on my face as I wrapped my arms around her and gently kissed her neck. *Mostly* false.

I felt Clarisse shudder in my arms and the look of fury that crossed Shannon's face seemed to suck the warmth from the room.

"Get away from that *bitch!*"

"Sister, he goads you. Do not start what you cannot finish." Chuck put his hand over Shannon's arm, visibly calming her.

Well, damn. Guess I got to up my game.

"Is this alright?" I whispered so softly into Clarisse's ear, I doubted that Shannon or her brother could hear even with their super-hearing.

I felt her nod almost imperceptibly. I ran my hands down her back and over her butt. I winked at Shannon as I squeezed. I admit, I felt guilty using Clarisse like that, but then again I also liked the feel of her butt. I tried not to throw up as an image of Jess popped into my head. Barfing would just ruin the whole effect and foil my evil plan.

Shannon literally shook with rage. Her brother moved both hands to her shoulders, keeping his sister from attacking and killing either or both of us.

Clarisse pulled back, looked me dead in the eye, and leaned in for a kiss. I almost panicked until I saw her wink at me as her lips touched mine. She had caught onto the game and was working with me. I hoped.

Her lips parted and I felt her tongue part mine. The kiss turned into more than just a kiss. Her arms wrapped around me and crushed me against her. For a moment I forgot about the mall, the bad guys, the problems we faced, life in general, any thoughts of survival, and pretty much everything else that ran through my brain on a daily basis. My hands squeezed the flesh of her behind as her tongue assaulted mine.

Until Shanria screamed.

I looked up just as she shattered her human seeming and swelled upward into her true Chosen form. I had seen it once. Months ago, we had fought to first blood in the streets outside the school. She stood nearly eight feet tall and had been the epitome of beauty. It was no wonder that mortals who had seen us in our true form had thought us gods. Among the most beautiful, Shanria had stood out beyond them.

That was not the creature that stood before us now.

Still eight feet tall, she towered above the rest of us, but gone were her wings of silver white feathers. Gone was her snow white hair and perfect skin. Gone were her robes of gossamer silver. Tattered leathery wings of black sprouted from her back. She looked almost like one of the Fallen, but even in their supposedly cursed forms they were beautiful. Clarisse had scales that looked almost like enameled plates in beautiful hues. Her leathery wings were whole and majestic. Shannon looked nothing like us.

Her skin was bloated and pocked with scars and wounds. Holes were torn in her wings. Twisted, gnarled horns sprouted from her head. Her mouth had become a twisted nest of broken fangs. She was *hideous* and more than a little scary. Even her brother let out gasp and separated himself from her.

"Sister!" His words fell on misshapen deaf ears as she screeched again and attacked. Her once beautiful flaming sword appeared, rusted in her gross-looking claws.

I stood dumbfounded, not believing what I was seeing. As she swung her sword, Clarisse's stopped it inches from my head.

"Connor! Snap out of it."

I shook my head and called my blades. Shannon's attention had been taken by Clarisse. She snarled and turned to fight her new opponent. The one who had stolen the object of her misguided affection.

You could feel the hatred flowing off of her in waves. She punched at Clarisse's blocks with short jabs of her wicked looking blade as her brother stood by and looked revolted.

I swung my blade at the exposed flesh between her wings, all thoughts of contracts and wars forgotten. My blade banished itself before it ever struck her. I stared at my empty hand in further disbelief.

Tired of the games, Shanria smacked aside Clarisse's blade, brought her arm back, and struck at Clarisse's chest. I leapt and brought my sword down in a sweeping arc, meaning to drive her blade aside. My sword and her sword passed through each other like optical illusions. Shanria's blade however pierced Clarisse's chest and came out her back.

I screamed. Everything stopped. Clarisse looked up at me with sad eyes and whispered, "You broke bread with her. You cannot harm her." Her eyes closed and she dropped like a sack of flour, pulling herself from Shanria's blade with a wet *plop*. She collapsed to the ground.

I found myself screaming a second time in a matter of moments. I dropped to my knees, not believing my friend was gone. The blade had gone through her heart.

Tears streamed down my face. Shannon began chuckling evilly as she wiped the blood of my friend against her tattered clothes. I looked at her brother at a loss. He couldn't take his hatred filled eyes from that of his sister. I could see he no longer considered her family. He turned and began to walk away, leaving me alone with the monster she had become.

I let the hatred consume every thought I had. It started deep within me and filled me completely. Finally it threatened to overflow human form.

The burst of magic stopped Cabriel in his tracks and he turned to look at me. His eyes opened in surprise. I didn't have scales, but my skin was tinged blue. My hair flowed white from my head and hung nearly to my waist. My eyes would not only be glowing red, they would be like rubies embedded within my face, leaving no whites showing. I could see the smaller blue-spiraled horns protruding from my head.

I stood up from the ground, casting one quick glance at my friend. I held out my hands to my side and channeled my fury, causing them to erupt into flames which coalesced into balls of torrential fire. With one last scream, I hurled them at Shanria.

The explosion that followed rocked the foundation of the mall. Flames engulfed all of us. Smoke filled the Winter Wonderland and the overhead sprinkler system came on, dousing the flames and clearing the air.

When we could see again, Shannon lay on the floor of the burned village. White snow turned to ash as she huddled in her crumpled human form, two holes burned clean through her chest. I took a few paces to close the distance between us and tried to roll her over with my foot. She crumpled to ash.

It was over.

Or so I thought. A clap of thunder boomed throughout the mall as several Chosen appeared, as well as several Fallen. I recognized Agravius of the Sages and Jun of the Warriors, as well as Darius and Mr. James.

"What have you done?" Darius was the first to speak as he eyed the remains of the Chosen. His eyes then settled on Clarisse and he rushed to her side. I didn't have the heart to tell him that I had gotten his daughter killed.

The Chosen gathered all called their weapons forth. Surprisingly enough, Cabriel held up his hand, staying their weapons. "He did not do this. Shanria had lost her senses. He merely defended himself. Read his memories if you must."

I stared at him like he was as crazy as his sister.

"Is this true, young one?" Agravius strode forward and looked me in the eyes.

I opened my mind and let him see exactly what had transpired. He nodded in understanding.

"Cabriel is correct. Judge for yourselves."

So I stood as Mr. James strode forth, and then the Chosen followed. They all dug through my mind and got the answers they wanted or needed.

"Let us depart," one of the Chosen spoke. "No laws were broken by the youngling. No Chosen died."

Then I understood. Shannon had changed. She had not become one of the Fallen, she had become something much, much worse. Her people had abandoned her imperfection and did not consider her death as a slight against them. To my dying day, I would never understand the thought processes of the Chosen. At least we had averted the war. At the cost of my friend.

The tears began falling as I turned and kneeled next to Darius. He held his hand over the gaping wound in Clarisse's chest.

Her eyes fluttered, she coughed and groaned, and sat up.

"What happened?"

"You freaking scared the shit out of me, that's what happened," I said and began sobbing. She laughed and hugged me close.

Sean Hayden

Epilogue

I stood next to Jess in my backyard. I wrapped my arm around her and pulled her into my shoulder, where she rested her head and gave me a content smile. I gave her a gentle kiss on the forehead and looked at my sister.

My parents had gone out for an impromptu dinner. Or so they thought. The truth is, I had given them a fifty-dollar gift certificate to Red Lobster and a pair of movie tickets and told them to get the hell out of the house with a bit of mind magic. Now a smart teenage boy would have done all this to have the party of the century at his house. Not me. I did it to make my sister happy.

She wanted nothing more in the world than to be human again. The only way to do it would be to sell her soul to the Fallen to get what she wanted. I thought the price was too steep. She didn't agree. She won the argument though and here we were.

Elizabeth and Cae sat at the ancient wrought-iron table on our back patio. Liz held Cae's hand while she scribbled a note in her own blood on a piece of notebook paper. I knew what the words said. I could feel each one in my bones as she wrote them. They were the same ones I had written a short time ago in my blood. They were the words that changed my world.

Sean Hayden

I gave Jess another kiss while we waited for her to finish. Clarisse stood above her and supervised, whispering each word to her softly before she wrote them.

By the time she was finished, the sun was setting. I reached into my hoodie pocket and pulled out my black candle. I didn't know why I kept it, but I did. I was actually a little glad. They were a complete bitch to find and it was my little contribution to this endeavor, since there wasn't any way in hell they would let me perform the magic. I'd probably turn her into an ultra-human or something. I'll admit it, too. The thought of having my normal human bratty sister back made me smile. Plus it would make her happy.

I gently let go of Jess and walked over to the table, setting the candle down in front of my sister. Clarisse handed her a lighter. Cae took it, lit the wick and the air around us stilled. It was like time stopped. The wick caught and the candle burned merrily. Cae began reciting the words she had written in her blood from memory and touched the paper to the flame. It went up in a puff of smoke. The candle went out and my sister stood and faced Clarisse.

"Are you ready?"

Cae nodded.

"Okay, wormette. What is it you wish for more than anything else in the world?"

"I wish to be one of the Fallen…"

There was a clap of thunder and the winds picked up.

Little sisters suck.

Did You Like This Book?

If you did and want to see more of Connor, Caelyn, and the rest of the crew, please… Leave a review!

About the Author

Born the son of a fire chief, Sean naturally developed a love of playing with fire. His family and friends quickly found other outlets for his destructive creativity. Writing is his latest endeavor.

Always a fan of the macabre, mythical, and magical, Sean found a love of urban fantasy and horror. After writing several novels in this genre, he found, fell in love with, and immersed himself in steampunk. He has always wanted to rewrite history and steampunk gave him that opportunity.

Sean currently lives in Florida as a fiber-optic engineer as well as an author. He was blessed with the two most amazing children he could ever hope for, has met the absolute love of his life, who coincidentally is his partner in everything. His hobbies include grand designs on world domination as well as a starring role in his own television sitcom.

www.seanhayden.org

www.ingramcontent.com/pod-product-compliance
Lightning Source LLC
Chambersburg PA
CBHW060545180626
46817CB00002B/728